FIDDLESTICKS AND FIRESTONES

Stephen Moore lives in Newcastle upon Tyne with his wife, his young son and his cat (the cat disputes this, and claims that *they* all live with *her*). He spent several years happily lost in the strange old world of museums, working as an exhibition and graphic designer. Until, that is, one day he discovered the magic that is storytelling . . .

FIDDLESTICKS AND FIRESTONES is his second novel for children. SPILLING THE MAGIC, his first, is published by Hodder Children's Books.

Fiddlesticks and Firestones

Stephen Moore

Hodder
Children's
Books

a division of Hodder Headline plc

The author would like to acknowledge with thanks the help
given by Northern Arts during the writing of this book.

First published in Great Britain in 1996
by Hodder Children's Books

A Catalogue record for this book is available
from the British Library

ISBN 0-340-66099-6

Typeset by Avon Dataset Ltd, Bidford-on-Avon

Printed and bound in Great Britain by
Cox & Wyman, Reading, Berks

Hodder Children's Books
A division of Hodder Headline plc
338 Euston Road
London NW1 3BH

For Robert and Hazel Moore

CONTENTS

CONTENTS

Knock Knock, Who's There?

Sometimes I hate grown-ups. They just sort of get in the way of everything. It wasn't my fault our mam came clomping down the stairs, *just* when I was right in the middle of the very first spell I'd ever done. I'm just a learner, you see, at spell-making, that is. The proper, magic stuff. It wasn't on purpose. I didn't *mean* to do it to her. Didn't *mean* to turn her into, into . . . well, I still don't know exactly what it was. I stuck her in an empty jam-jar with a piece of lettuce, and poked holes in the lid so that she could breathe.

Hang on though, I'm getting ahead of myself – real adventures don't start in the exciting places. Real adventures start on dead boring, drizzly dull Thursday mornings. Or at least, this one did. It was at that funny time halfway through the summer holidays, when nothing ever happens, when nothing is the tiniest bit interesting, and you could almost wish to be back at school. I was stuck in the living room with our Mary, waiting for drippy Wendy Milligan – Fiddlesticks Milligan – to bang on the front door . . .

'And you'll play nicely with her, the pair of you,' Mam's voice threatened, on her way up the stairs. 'Can you two hear me in there? Are you listening?'

'Ye-es, Mam,' Mary huffed.

'Billy? Billy Tibbet? You're the eldest. Don't go skulking off the minute she gets here. Leaving it all to Mary.'

'Ye-es, Mam.'

'Pardon?'

'I mean no-o, Mam.'

'And you've tidied up that room, like I told you?'

'Ye-es, Mam.' Huh. We hadn't. I liked our house the way it was, with a comfortable layer of dust over everything. Not really dirty, just enough to make you feel at home. And anyway, the living room was where we kept all our interesting stuff. You know, like my bottle tops and Mary's rag dolls. The junk our dad rescues from car-boot sales, and Mam's knitting patterns cut out of hundred-year-old magazines, with pictures of women on the back advertising knickers the size of our garden. Oh, all that kind of stuff. I didn't see why it should all be cleared up just because we were having a rotten visitor.

'I told Mrs Milligan mind, said you'd both be really pleased to help out.' Mam had reached the bathroom. 'Having somebody to play with will help young Wendy take her mind off things. Now that her dad's . . . now that her dad's . . .' Her voice got stuck there, and she started clattering shampoo bottles about in the bathroom cabinet, like it was all some big, grown-up secret. Well, it wasn't.

'Now that her dad's done a bunk,' I said, 'with that Kathleen Ferguson's mam, from Raby Street.'

'I suppose we wouldn't like it, Billy,' Mary said, 'if our dad did something like that.'

'Huh. Our dad's got more sense, hasn't he? Flippin' Fiddlesticks Milligan, coming here. Nobody likes her. Nobody in the whole wide world.'

11

I suppose I should tell you why. Well, for a start she's as thin as a spelk, with tiny little weaselly eyes, and a sort of whimpering, wet-watery voice. Everything she says sounds like a complaint. And she stands funny, with her legs mixed up, always twiddling with her hair and pulling at the bottom of her dress, like she's bursting for the bog. That's why she's nicknamed Fiddlesticks. Then, there's her allergies, and her diseases – if she's not scratching something, she's catching something. There's always something wrong with her. And if you still need convincing, I'll tell you something else. She's useless, absolutely useless, *at everything*. Couldn't get herself picked for the school sports if she was the only one to turn up! Huh, I could go on for ever about Fiddlesticks Milligan. But I won't, because that's when the banging on the front door started.

'I'm not answering it,' Mary said, shaking her head, stuffing it deeper into the book she was pretending to read.

'Well, I'm not answering it either,' I said.

Nobody moved.

The banging came again.

'Mary! Billy! Will one of you two *p-lease* answer that door. Before I have to come down there and knock your heads together,' Mam whispered down the stairs, at the top of her voice, if you know what I mean. She was really good at doing that.

The banging on the door was getting frantic.

I glared daggers at Mary. 'Mam said your name first.' *Firsts* was a sort of unwritten rule. Mary tried glaring back, but she knew she'd lost.

I heard the front door open. I heard Mary's muffled hello, and the weak, wet-watery reply. Fiddlesticks Milligan all right. I was out of the living room, and into the cupboard under the stairs before she was over the front step. I stuck my ear to the cupboard door, and listened.

'I hope there's no cats in here,' Fiddlesticks whined. 'I can't have cats in the house. Their fur makes me itch. I come out in huge red blotches and my skin flakes off.'

'No, there's no cats,' Mary said, wearily. 'Our Mog's been shut up in the garden shed.' The

13

sound of shuffling feet and muffled voices disappeared into the living room.

I relaxed a bit, leant backwards in the dusty grey darkness, perched myself between the vacuum cleaner and the row of winter coats that smelled reassuringly of Mam and Dad. Waited for a chance to make a proper escape.

The banging on the front door started up again! But even louder and harder than before, and in a desperate hurry. And whoever it was this time, they weren't using the knocker. They were banging on the wood-work. Our mam would go wild if they were making marks.

I didn't wait for Mam to start screaming blue murder. I stormed out of the cupboard and across the hall, and yanked the door open. I'd catch the silly beggars.

There was nobody there.

I was ready to boil over, to thump some-body. Huh, there wasn't a single person in the whole of our street.

Outside a sharp wind was playing about with the drizzle, and the front path was shining, streaked with tiny, blue-green rainbows. Where Fiddlesticks had walked there were squelchy, rubbery smudges. But there were no other footprints. Nobody else had been up our path in yonks. It didn't make any sense, so I gave up and shut the door again. Or at least, I nearly did. As I swung it to, I noticed something sitting on the doorstep – a small brown paper parcel, tied up with string. The parcel was an odd shape, round and flat at the same time, as if somebody had wrapped up a lump of Plasticine.

I bent down, picked it up. There wasn't a name on it, or an address, a stamp or anything. The wrapping paper felt as thick as cardboard, and was all cracked and crumbly. And the string wasn't string, it was more like a stiff, dry leather. Dry, even in the rain. Maybe I should have been more careful. But well, if there was nothing on the parcel to say that it was for me, there was nothing on the parcel to say that it wasn't. So I tore it open, snapped the leather string, let the wind carry the wrapping out of my hand and off up the street.

Inside the first wrapper there was a second

wrapper, bound tightly around something hard in the middle. There was writing on it: WARNING. DO NOT OPEN THIS PACKAGE WITHOUT READING THESE INSTRUCT— That's all I read. I was being so pigheaded I just ripped the wrapper off, and let it follow the first one up the street in the wind.

All that was left in my hand was a stone. A blue stone, perfectly smooth and with two small holes running through it. (It was a bit like two big, funny-coloured Polo mints stuck together, but with all the letters sucked off).

'Oowww! Ooooo!' I yelped, or screamed, or something. The stone had suddenly turned red hot. A really daft kind of red hot! And a tingling, fizzy buzziness of pain shot through my fingers, up my arm, around the inside of my head and back again, scalding my tongue on the way, jabbing my teeth like a dentist's drill.

Then, suddenly, our front door and our garden disappeared, along with the drizzly dull Thursday morning and the whole of the rest of the world. In its place stretched a darkness so

deep and heavy I could almost feel its touch.
But, it wasn't an empty darkness – there was a
vague outline . . . the even deeper, darker,
threatening shape of a mountain . . . a huge
great mountain, with someone, something,
standing alone at the top. The figure didn't
move, just stood there, still as a statue.
Waiting . . .

I must have screamed again.

'Billy? Billy? What's the matter?' Mary
came charging up our hall, pushing past me,
fists closed ready to thump. And Fiddlesticks
was trailing along behind her, sticking her neb
in.

'Did you see it Mary? Did you see?' I said.

'What, Billy? What, where?'

'There! Right there in front of you, stupid.
The mountain, and *him*!' I could feel myself
getting more and more angry. Our Mary was
starting to make silly faces – and worse, so was
Fiddlesticks Milligan. Faces that said pull the
other one, Billy, it's got bells on.

'It *was* there,' I cried.

Nothing to see now, though. Just the front
garden. Just me, standing on the doorstep in

the rain, with a small blue stone clutched in my hand. I held it up, wanted Mary to see, wanted her to understand . . .

But that was when our mam came thumping down the stairs, with half her make-up slopped across her face. 'What on earth are you two doing to this poor lass?' she said, putting an arm around Fiddlesticks, jumping to wrong conclusions. 'Can't I trust you on your own for five minutes!'

'It's all right, Mam,' Mary sniggered. 'It's just our Billy, being silly.'

I scowled at her. Scowled at them all. And if, inside my head, I had them all turning into something really really nasty and horrible, then maybe they deserved it. It's at times like that you're never really sure how things happen. In my hand the blue stone flickered, and grew warm again. Grew stinging hot. I didn't know what it meant. I didn't know what I was doing. I didn't!

'What have you got there, Billy?' Mam asked, in her best guilty-before-being-proved-innocent voice. 'Let me see—'

Too late. Too ruddy late.

My very last scowl must have landed on her, because that's when it happened. That's when I turned our mam into, into . . .

'Where – where's your mam gone, Billy?' Fiddlesticks squirmed and pulled at the bottom of her dress. 'And – urgh! – what's *that* crawling across the carpet? I think I'm going to be sick.'

'What have you done, Billy?' Mary shrieked. 'What have you done to Mam?'

'Shut up, Mary. Just shut up,' I cried. 'Don't you dare say anything. Not either of you. Not ever.'

'Bring her back, then. Quickly.'

I looked at the cold blue stone in my hand. Looked at the Mam-thing. Looked at the stone again. Fiddlesticks wasn't the only one feeling sick. 'I – I can't. I don't know how.'

'Oh, Billy—'

I flung the stone across the hall, heard it clack-clack against the far wall as it broke in two. As if throwing it away, smashing it, could somehow put everything right, could make me feel better. Well, it couldn't.

The Mam-thing was squatting uncomfortably

19

in the middle of the hall carpet, rocking herself gently backwards and forwards. And I knew, just knew that if she'd still been our proper mam, there'd have been clouts around ear-holes.

'It's horrible. It's got sharp teeth, *and fur*,' Fiddlesticks whined, in her wet-watery voice, twisting up her face ready to blubber. 'I want to go home!'

'She's not horrible at all,' I said. I knelt down and carefully stroked the tiny Mam-thing with a finger. 'See? She's really quite . . . quite nice. And anyway, *you're* not going anywhere.' I didn't grab hold of her. Just made a fist. Just looked.

'You can't keep me here, Billy Tibbet. That's kidnap. And I'm getting a rash. I know I am.' Fiddlesticks started jigging up and down, scratching at her arms and legs. 'My cousin's dad's in the poliss. He'll send you both to prison. Prob'ly for ever. Prob'ly won't ever let you out again.'

'Oh, shut up and stand still, will you. You're frightening our mam,' Mary said. 'Do you think we should find her something to eat? Y'know,

20

Billy, some grass, or some lettuce, or something?'

I shrugged. The Mam-thing stopped rocking. Curled herself up into a blodgy, huffy ball, and wouldn't come out again.

TWO

The Secret

Putting our mam in a jam-jar – for safe keeping and that – well, that was my idea. But blabbing secrets to Fiddlesticks Milligan, that was our Mary. What secrets? I'd better tell you if you don't already know. All this weird magic stuff, it's happened to us before. And you see, we have got a secret. Not a stupid made-up kids' game, either. But a *real* secret, that's just about impossible to believe. Even in a billion years.

I was busy tying a string handle to the Mam-thing's jam-jar, and Fiddlesticks was busy getting in the way, poking her nose against the glass for a better look, and well . . . Mary just walked into the kitchen and blurted it out. 'I knew!' she said, bursting with excitement. 'I knew! This is all Murn's doing, isn't it?' She had the two pieces of the blue stone cupped carefully in her open hands, and there was a funny look stuck to her face. A look that made her seem older somehow, full of questions, full of answers too. 'Billy? I'm right, aren't I?'

'Murn?' said Fiddlesticks, twiddling with her hair. 'What's Murn?'

'Shut up, Mary,' I shouted. 'Not in front of *her*. That's secret. That's *our* secret.'

'But, Billy, where did you find it?'

'It was in a parcel, on the front step, after that banging on the door. But I said, Mary, just shut up. It's got nothing to do with *her*.'

'I don't want to play your silly games, anyway,' Fiddlesticks huffed.

'This is not a game,' Mary said, her voice suddenly quiet and serious.

'Mary, no!'

'Well, it's not a game, is it, Billy? Not if it's really from Murn. And anyway, she's already in it. She saw everything.'

In the end, I suppose we had to tell her, couldn't really not.

'You've got to promise, mind, never, *ever*, EVER to breathe a word of this to anyone.' I twisted both of Fiddlesticks' ears until she squeaked.

'Ow! Oow! No, I won't. I won't.'

''Cos if you do, if you do—' I gave her ears another twist.

'I promise,' she whined. 'I promise.'

'Right then, right. You see, Murn's a place . . . well, more than that. Murn's a whole world.'

'A what?'

'A *world*! Now just listen, will you.' I twisted her ears again, just to make sure. 'Murn's like . . . like this world where we live, only it's somewhere else. And it's different. There's a moon, instead of a sun. And it's full of mountains – ninety-seven of them, floating about in space. And, and it's magic there, with real dragons and pigs that can fly and—'

'Oh yes. And I suppose there's witches and wizards too,' Fiddlesticks sniggered.

'Well, that just shows what you know, doesn't it, because there are. Except in Murn they're called Spellbinders.'

'Spellbinders? Huh! You've both been watching too much telly.'

'Yes, but *real* Spellbinders,' I said. 'Our Aunt Lilly's one of them.'

'Oh, ha ha, very funny.' Fiddlesticks sniggered again. 'I don't remember seeing her on the *Six O'Clock News*.'

Huh, I couldn't explain it any better, even if it did sound daft. And Fiddlesticks Milligan couldn't stop sniggering. 'Oh, you try and tell her, sis.'

Mary looked down at the broken stone in her hand. 'Murn's a place for adventures,' she said, her eyes sparkling, like she was on fire inside. 'Wonderful, wonderful adventures. And it's real. And we're not making it up. We've been there, haven't we, Billy?' I was nodding frantically.

For a moment Fiddlesticks' face was a copy of Mary's – alight and fiery. Huh, just for a moment, though. 'You know what?' she said, suddenly remembering herself. 'That's the biggest heap of rubbish I've ever heard in my whole life.'

'It is not rubbish!' Mary snapped. 'Where do you think this came from?' She pushed the broken stone right under Fiddlesticks' nose. 'And how else can you explain what's happened to our mam?'

'Oh, that thing in the jam-jar's nothing

special. Haven't you heard of pet shops? 'Spect it's some kind of ornamental hamster. Just wait till I tell the class at school—'

'You're not snitching to anyone!' Mary warned. She'd had enough of Fiddlesticks Milligan, and there might have been a really nasty fight then. But there wasn't.

Suddenly, a bright blue spark jumped out of the back of my dad's radio, turned into a miniature firework display, and exploded across the ceiling. Scared the living daylights out of us. The radio was sitting on the kitchen window-sill, wasn't even plugged in. Its buttons flicked up, flicked down, then up again, and it crackled and spat, like it was waking up.

And then, the radio spoke to us.

— THREE —

The Kettle and the Radio

'Er, hello,' said the radio. 'Hello, is there anybody there?'

'Eeeeeee! What's happening?' Fiddlesticks squealed.

'What's that? Speak up. This is not a very good line. Are you receiving me? Er, over.'

'Hello,' Mary said, cautiously. 'Hello?'

'Is that you, Mary dear?'

'Um, yes. Yes it is.'

'Oh, splendid, splendid. And how are you?'

'Very well, thank you,' Mary said, her voice sounding funny, as if she'd just bumped into the Queen or something.

'Oh, this is wonderful. I wasn't sure I could still do it. Now then, your brother Billy, how is he?'

'Very well, thank you.'

'Splendid, splendid.'

Suddenly, the kettle, which had been standing quietly on the bench next to the sink, exploded into life. 'Ka! For goodness sake, woman, will you get to the point. Some people have got battles to fight.' The kettle was huffing and puffing at the radio, showering the room with jets of steam.

Our kettle was yelling at my dad's radio. *Our kettle was yelling at my dad's radio!*

The radio clicked and jittered awkwardly, sputtering blue sparks everywhere. 'Don't you speak to me like that,' it said.

'Ka! Let me have a go, then. Let me speak to them.'

There was a sudden muffled, thudding stomping sound, and then the radio squawked, 'Don't you dare touch that! This is my spell. You'll, you'll only break it!' Another flurry of blue sparks burst out of the radio and drifted up to the ceiling.

The radio and the kettle went very still, and quiet. And stayed that way.

I stared at our Mary. There was something oddly familiar about those voices. Even if they had come out of a radio and a kettle. 'Do you know what I think?' I said. She did.

'Spellbinders,' she said, her face bursting

into a huge grin. 'It's Murdle Clay and Idrik Sirk. I'm sure. The Spellbinders of Murn.' She gave Fiddlesticks such a look, you know, as if to say I told you so.

'I don't want to play this game any more,' Fiddlesticks whined. 'I just want to go home.'

There wasn't time to tell her to shut up, because the kettle began to bubble and steam again. Hissing and fizzing wildly as it began to speak. 'Ka! There, see? I've done it, woman. I told you I could.' There was a short, smug silence (and I'm sure someone, somewhere, was grinning to themselves). 'Now then, Mary, can you still hear me?'

'Yes,' Mary said, shyly.

'Ka! Speak up, girl,' spat the kettle. 'We can't keep this spell going for ever. This is no easy bind.'

'Yes, I can hear you,' she shouted.

'Good. And Billy, is Billy there?'

'Yes. Yes, I can hear,' I shouted at the kettle.

'Make it stop. Please, make it stop,' Fiddlesticks cried, in a snively whisper, before disappearing under the kitchen table. Luckily, nobody seemed to hear.

'And you found your Twitch, dear. Your Firestone? With the set of instructions?' crackled the radio.

'My . . . *my* Twitch?' I said.

'Yes, dear. The blue Firestone. It did arrive, didn't it?'

'I er, I, I . . .' I couldn't speak. And there was a whoppin' great lump of ice filling my stomach.

That got Fiddlesticks Milligan up from under the table. 'What's this Twitch then, Billy?' she said.

'It's a . . . it's a . . .'

'If you must know,' Mary snapped, 'it's what Spellbinders use to keep all their spells and knowledge and special stuff in.'

'Eh?'

'You know, it's like a notebook, or a computer. Only this Twitch is a stone.'

Fiddlesticks looked down her nose thoughtfully, like she didn't believe a word of it, but was thinking it all over anyway. Then she smirked, turned to the radio, and snitched. 'Billy got that all right. He got your Twitch – thing. But you know what? He

30

ripped up the instructions.' The radio and the kettle were listening intently now. 'And you know what else? Then he threw the stone away. Bust it. Bust it into a million-billion tiny little pieces.'

The radio crackled and snapped noisily, and the kettle stopped blowing steam out, and started sucking it in instead. Like a huge gasp of breath.

'No, I didn't,' I said, denying everything.

'Oh, yes he did.'

'And anyway, even if I did break it – it was just into two bits.'

'And you should see what he's done to his mam an' all!'

The silence then was horrible. Nothing moved or whirred, fizzed or clicked. Just an empty silence, filling up with anger, filling up with sadness and worry, all at the same time . . .

And I wanted to be yelled at. I wanted the Spellbinders to tell me what a stupid, ungrateful, nasty little child I was. Wanted the lecture that told me how great a gift the Firestone was. How the 'Binders had made it specially for me. How it was magic. How, by rights, only a proper 'Binder could have one. How – well, I know all that stuff now.

In the end, a voice did break the silence. A slow quiet voice, matter-of-fact and deadly serious. Like a teacher, when you haven't done your homework, when you've used up all your chances and you still haven't done your homework. 'Two must make one, Billy boy,' said the kettle. 'And without instruction the secrets of a 'Binder's magic must be learnt the hard way.'

'Quickly now. Quickly, Idrik,' the radio interrupted. 'The spell's unwinding. And they are about to attack again!'

'Listen up, boy,' the kettle spat, urgently. 'Murn's in deadly trouble. The tide turns against us. The hunt may have already started.' There were bloops and bleeps and dangerous electric-sounding fizzes before the voice managed to break through again. 'We need your help.' His voice was fading away. 'But remember, friends wait in the unlikeliest of places.' There were more bloops and bleeps and yelps of static. But nothing else. Just a radio and a kettle, and a dreadful silence.

'But, but what help? What trouble? What

tide?' Mary yelled at the kettle. 'And what hunt? You haven't explained anything at all yet!'

I picked up the radio and shook it until something started to rattle about loose inside. As if I could somehow empty out the answers. Well, I couldn't.

FOUR

The Would-be Spellbinders

We laid our evidence on the kitchen table, and sat looking at it. There was the kettle, and the radio, the Mam-thing still curled up tight in her jam-jar, and the broken blue stone. The Fire-stone. Nothing very special-looking about it, now. The pieces were about the same size, and they both had a hole running through them, like the beads of a necklace. They weren't warm to touch or anything. No. They were cold, as cold as . . . well, as cold as stone, I suppose.

'They put some funny stuff on the radio,' said Fiddlesticks, shuffling about in her chair to get a better look at our evidence. 'None of it made any sense.'

'It wasn't a radio programme, stupid,' I said. 'It was a *real* message.'

'Oh yes, I forgot. We're pretending this is real, aren't we.'

'When was the last time you heard a kettle

talking to a radio?' Mary snapped.

'They can do anything these days – with special effects,' huffed Fiddlesticks. ''Spect that's all it was. 'Spect it's dead easy.'

'Didn't you take in a single word we told you?' I said.

'All that silly Murn rubbish.'

'We've told you a billion times, it is not rubbish!' I could have thumped her.

'All right then,' she said. 'If it's not rubbish, who was that Murdle Clay?'

'I said, she's a Spellbinder. She's our aunt.'

'You told me your aunt was called Lilly.' Fiddlesticks was smirking now.

'She was our old Aunt Lilly when she lived here! It was a kind of secret identity. In Murn she's called Murdle Clay. It's simple enough!'

'And Idrik Sirk, he's a Spellbinder too?'

'Yes,' Mary said. 'Yes. Except, um . . . except he's a dead one. He's just a skeleton. Murdle Clay probably had to do a special spell to fetch him up out of his tomb.'

'Urgh! Now you are making it up. Just trying to frighten me because I won't believe you.'

'No we're not,' Mary said, and as she spoke

her voice went all funny, like she was remembering a favourite dream. 'Idrik Sirk isn't at all frightening. Not when he's on your side. I like him.'

'And it's all *really* true?'

'Yes.'

Fiddlesticks wasn't going to give in. 'Even if it is true, the radio said *hunting*. I don't want to go hunting. It's nasty and cruel and bloody. And how would you like it if somebody hunted you?'

Mary picked up a piece of the Firestone and twiddled it between her fingers. Nothing happened. I didn't even expect it to. 'If only you hadn't broken the Firestone, Billy,' she sighed. 'If only you'd read those rotten instructions.'

I didn't bother to answer. I'd had enough. We were getting nowhere, very fast, and the three of us sulking moodily around the kitchen table wasn't going to help. 'Listen, Murn needs our help!' I said, squeaking angrily. 'What we need are ideas. We've got to find a way to get there.'

'Well, two pieces of broken stone,' Fiddlesticks said, matter-of-factly.

Mary sighed. 'What?'

'Two pieces of broken stone,' Fiddlesticks said, again. 'I just thought . . . that Idrik-Sirk-kettle-whatsit said something about two must make one. 'Spect we've got to put the stone back together again. Y'know, with sticky tape or glue.'

'Oh, don't be so stupid, Fiddlesticks. You can't stick magic together with glue.'

Huh. In the end, we did try. Didn't work, though. Not even with the super-duper-stick-anything-to-anything-even-in-a-driving-thunderstorm kind of stuff. We just got glue everywhere. 'There must be some way of making the stone work,' I said, trying to wipe the glue off my hands with the tablecloth.

'You're the one who turned our mam into a ball of fur.' Mary picked up the jam-jar and slammed it down again. 'You must remember how you did it.'

'Well, I don't.'

'Not anything, Billy?' Fiddlesticks asked.

'No. I unwrapped the Firestone and held it in my hand. Then it started to get hot, glowed and that. And when Mam came down the stairs . . .

zonk!' It was my turn to pick up the jam-jar, and slam it down hard.

'Oh, you must have done something else,' Mary said. 'Think, Billy! Think!'

Think. That work stuck in my head. Stuck there, wouldn't go away again. Think . . . *Think*.

'Y'know, Mary, that's it!' I said. 'Think! That's what else I did. It might sound daft, but I was holding the stone, and . . . I was thinking. That's how it must work.'

'You mean you thought *that* up?' Fiddlesticks poked her finger at the jam-jar.

'I was in a bad mood.'

'All right then. If thinking makes the stone work, and we can't fix it or anything, where does "two must make one, Billy boy" come into it?'

'That's a cinch!' I waited a moment, just to see if she'd clicked on. She hadn't. 'Look, one stone, one of me, and the magic worked. So-o. Two stones must need two people. Two makes one. See?'

'I'm not sure I want to make the magic work,' Fiddlesticks said, twiddling her hair. 'It's too dangerous. You don't know what you're doing. And you're just guessing at everything.'

'Don't you want to have an adventure in Murn?' I said.

'No,' she said, getting ready to snivel again. 'No, I don't. I just want to go home.'

'Listen, if we say you're *in*, then you're *in*!' Mary snapped, eager to get on. 'We can't leave our mam stuck in a jam-jar for ever. And anyway, if me and Billy keep the stones you won't have to do anything.'

I was already on my feet, getting stuff ready for Murn and that. I handed the jam-jar to Mary. 'Here, I think you'd better look after Mam. We're taking her with us. Getting a proper Spellbinder to sort her out.'

Next, I emptied her canvas school bag on to the floor.

'Careful, Billy, that's got my summer projects in it. What do you want it for, anyway?'

'Supplies,' I said. 'We'll need some proper supplies. We don't know what kind of help Murn wants, or for how long. And you know the kind of rotten stuff they try to feed you on there. Well, I want some real food this time!'

'What about Dad's radio, then?' Mary said.

'What?'

'We'd better take something. The 'Binders might want to send us another message.'

'And a proper first-aid kit,' Fiddlesticks said.

'And some paper tissues, for . . . you know, Billy.'

'Oh, all right. And I'll see if I can get the kitchen sink in as well, shall I?'

I raided the fridge and the bread bin. Stuffed the bag until it was bursting with doorstep sandwiches and bottles of pop. 'Here, Fiddlesticks, get a hold of this bag. I'm putting you in charge of supplies and communications.'

'I can't carry that, it's far too heavy for me. Anyway, don't see why I should. I'm the one's been kidnapped.'

I didn't say anything. Just hooked her arm through the strap of the bag and slung it across her back.

Lastly, I looped string through the holes of the broken Firestone. Made pendants out of them. I put one around my neck, and the other around Mary's. Then, it was time to go. Huh, if only we knew how . . .

I stood and faced our Mary, and took hold of my Firestone.

'But what should *I* do?' Fiddlesticks asked, sulkily.

'Just stand out of the way, and be ready,' I said.

'Ready for what?'

I ignored her, concentrated on Mary. 'Take hold of your Firestone, and think about Murn. That's it. Carefully though, we're not properly trained, we don't know the rules.' I closed my eyes, and as I did a whole bucketful of butterflies started dancing in my stomach. Were we really going back to Murn?

I waited for something unusual to happen.

It didn't.

'Are you thinking, Mary?'

'Yes.'

'Holding your stone?'

'Yes!'

Still nothing happened.

'Maybe Fiddlesticks has got to help,' I said, guessing. Yes, guessing. And you'd better get used to it. There's more ifs, buts and guesses in real adventures than anything else. 'We could all stand in a circle.'

'No,' said Mary, 'I think it should be a triangle.'

'All right. We'll stand in a triangle then. But come on—'

'Do I have to?' Fiddlesticks said, shuffling huffily across the floor, fiddling with the bottom of her dress.

'Yes, you do. Now, come on. Get ready . . . steady . . . *think!*'

Nothing happened. We must have stood there for ten minutes, but nothing happened.

'I might have known.' Fiddlesticks was whining again.

I looked at Mary. She was looking blankly at her Firestone. 'Maybe it's the thinking bit that's not quite right,' I said, still guessing. 'Maybe we've got to think about exactly the same thing, at exactly the same time. I mean – not just any old thing about Murn, but exactly the same thing.'

'Oh, that's just daft, Billy,' Mary snapped. 'How am I supposed to know what you're thinking?'

Fiddlesticks looked at me quizzically.

'I'll tell you what I'm going to think, stupid – that's how.'

'All right then, what *are* you going to think?'

'Er . . .' I hadn't really thought. 'A mountain,' I said. 'That's the easiest thing. Murn's full of mountains, and one of them is blue. You can both manage to think about a blue mountain without messing it up, can't you?'

Mary stuck her tongue out.

We didn't bother with triangles, just filled our heads with a picture of a blue mountain. And, at last my Firestone began to flicker, its strange warmth tickling the ends of my fingers. It was going to work. It really was going to work, this time!

Bzzzz-ZZzzooonnNKK!

'Urgh! Something sticky's dribbling on me. Ow! That hurts,' Fiddlesticks squeaked. 'Is *this* Murn, then?'

'Does it look like it, stupid?'

'I've never been there, so I don't know, do I?'

I could only just see. My eyes were smarting, like somebody had rubbed them with a piece of raw onion. We were all squashed up close together, on the inside of a very ordinary cupboard, with a row of smelly mops and buckets full of stinking disinfectant.

'Wherever it is, we don't want to be here!' I said, trying to rub the sting out of my eyes. 'Do the thinking bit again, but properly this time.'

Bzzzz-ZZzzooonnNKK!

'Ooooo! That scratched,' Mary yelped.

'And I've been bitten,' Fiddlesticks cried. 'Bitten to death.'

Now we were in the middle of some rotten prickly thorn bushes – the thorn bushes the gardener had planted behind our school gym to keep the kids off. 'Look, you two. Somebody's not thinking at all, are they?' I said, holding perfectly still. I could feel the thorns pressing in, like tiny little needles, all over me.

'Well, I am!' Mary snapped. 'It might be you, Billy.'

'It is not me!' I yelled, not caring who else heard. 'The pair of you'll just have to try harder.'

'I'm trying as hard as I can,' Fiddlesticks whined, her voice squeaking guiltily. 'I'm just not very good at this sort of thing. Other thoughts keep getting in the way.'

'Well, don't think them,' I said.

'They're already there, inside my head, so I

can't *not* think them.' Her eyes had started to leak.

'Maybe it's just the stone carriers who have to do the thinking bit, Billy?' Mary said. 'Maybe other people's thoughts just mess it all up.'

'Right then,' I said. (Anything was worth a try to get us out of those rotten bushes). 'From now on, Mary and me are doing ALL the thinking. And, Fiddlesticks, you're doing the – the *un*-thinking.'

'The *un*-thinking?'

'Yes. Just let that thing you call a brain go blank. And I mean completely blank.'

'I'll, I'll try,' she sniffed, and rubbed the tears off the end of her nose.

'Get ready . . . Now! I'm thinking about the blue mountain of Murn. The blue Mountain of Murn.'

Bzzzz-ZZzzooonnNKK!

A pair of angry green eyes were staring at me out of a thick, murky darkness. And an unfriendly, slobbering, gurgling noise was coming from somewhere close by.

'Fiddlesticks! I thought I told you to *un*-think!'

'Well, I – I just can't.' Now there were four pairs of green eyes, and stereo gurgles. And they were moving closer. 'I didn't want to come with you in the first place!'

'That's it!' Mary said.

'Eh?'

'Start thinking about home, Billy. Think about being back in our kitchen. We can't possibly get that wrong.'

'But that would mean starting the adventure all over again.'

'Oh, Please, Billy. Please,' cried Fiddlesticks. 'I'll *un*-think properly. I promise I will. Before those slobbering thingies get any closer.'

'Oh, all right. All right! I'm at home in the kitchen. At home in the kitchen.'

'Again, Billy, again!'

'I'M AT HOME IN THE KITCHEN.'

Bzzzz-ZZzzooonnNKK!

FIVE

The Door That Wasn't There

This time, the spell worked. Perfectly. There we were, the three of us, back sitting gloomily around the kitchen table. 'What now, Billy?' Mary said. 'If we're supposed to be helping Murn we're not getting very far, are we?'

'We could have one last go with the Firestone,' I said. Everybody groaned. Even the curled up Mam-thing in her jam-jar ground her teeth. I wasn't going to give up. 'But this time, instead of trying the rotten magic stuff ourselves, we could . . . we could just ask for help. You know, *proper* help. That is, unless somebody else has got a better plan?' I knew they hadn't.

Cautiously, we took hold of our Firestones. 'Fiddlesticks, are you *un*-thinking?'

'Yes,' she said. She shut her eyes, bit her lip, and scrunched up the bottom of her dress with the effort of getting it right.

'OK, Mary. Think, help. Nothing else, just

help. Say it with me. Help. Hel-p. Hel-p.'

'HEL-P. HEL-P. HEL-P.'

Bzzzz-ZZzzooonnn . . . We never got as far as *K!* Not this time.

There was a loud banging on our front door. Yes, banging on our front door, again! And right in the middle of our flippin' spell, this time. 'I don't believe this! Who the heck—' I glared at Mary, glared at Fiddlesticks.

'Don't go blaming us, Billy. Go and answer it!' I did, and I got there just in time too. Just as the banging *on* the door became a splintering thud *through* the door, and a hole as big as Christmas appeared in the middle.

Standing with its feet on our front doorstep – well, to be more accurate, with its trotters on our front doorstep – was a large pink pig. An old, battle-scarred pig, with an angry face, and wings. Yes, a pig with wings. And that wasn't all. Riding on his back was a small green man. I suppose I should have been surprised. I suppose I was, a little bit. But I wasn't shocked. You see, I've seen flying pigs before. Small green men too. Snooks they're called, a sort of cross between an elf, a goblin, and a tree trunk!

(But don't ever let them hear you say that).
Anyway, I might not have been shocked by
their sudden arrival, but they were.

'What place is this, Fellin Tappa? Surely
those we seek cannot be found here!' The flying pig reared up, thrashed the air angrily with
his wings, and bashed another hole in the door
with his trotters. Huh, so much for Mam's
paintwork.

'I fear so, Brock!' cried Fellin Tappa, clinging
tightly to the ears of the huge pig. 'There is
magic upon the air, though it's a poor weave!'

'Can . . . Can I help you?' I said.

Huh, they didn't answer, just ignored me, as
if I wasn't there. Instead, the flying pig hurled
himself into the air and darted around the far
side of the house. I didn't see what they did
there, but I heard the growls and curses. At last
they reappeared, looking even more angry, and
in a bigger flap than ever.

'Then it is true,' snorted the flying pig.

The snook took one hand off the flying pig's
ears, leant towards me, and poked his nose into
my face. 'A 'Binder's turn, is it?' he asked.

'Pardon?' I said.

'Did you send for us with magic? Did you use a calling spell?'

'Well, I might have done I suppose, but—' I would have explained properly, but he didn't give me the chance.

'Oh, bother! I thought so.' He gave a sort of nervous, guilty laugh, and then both the snook and the flying pig gave a long, low bow. 'Forgive our brashness, er, Master 'Binder? – but I fear the threading of your spell is already loose. If you have made a door that opens upon your own world, then you have made a door that opens upon Murn, and we must find the way at once!' With that, the flying pig lurched forward, puffing and blowing. He barged me out of his way, charged down our hall and into the kitchen.

'Hang on, you'd better wait for me,' I shouted after them, picking myself up off the floor. I heard Fiddlesticks' piercing, wet-watery shriek just as I reached the kitchen door.

'Urgh! It's monsters and aliens! Horrible, pink and green slimy aliens,' she screeched.

'They're not monsters. Or aliens,' Mary snapped back at her. Then she smiled a kind of worried, questioning smile at me. 'Billy?'

'This is our help. This is the help we asked for. I, er, I think.'

Fellin Tappa and Brock were flying circles around the room, swiping pans and mugs, and Mam's best china plates off the shelves as they went. The flying pig's dangling legs toppled the table and skittled the chairs like – well, like skittles.

And then, at last, Fellin Tappa seemed to find what he was searching for, and brought Brock to a gasping standstill at the far end of the kitchen. 'This *must* be it,' he said. 'Oh bother! Bother, bother! But where is the key? Must have the key.' The small green snook stopped being green, and started being a very sick-looking purply-grey colour. He pulled himself off the flying pig's back and poked his nose into Mary's face. 'I don't suppose you have the wrong key for this door?'

'What door?'

'He's a loony,' Fiddlesticks whined nervously, backing away towards the hall.

'This is the wrong world. And this is the wrong door in the wrong house. So we've got

51

to have the wrong key. Stands to reason.'

'Well, I've got my front-door key, if that's any help?' Mary suggested.

I shrugged.

'Oh yes, and how do you open the wrong door with the wrong key?' Fiddlesticks whined. 'Especially when there isn't even a door there in the first place.'

The snook eyed her suspiciously. 'Is she *really* on our side?' he asked. 'There are spies everywhere.' Fiddlesticks was going to start snivelling again, I just knew it.

'Look, have you got a key in your pocket?' I asked her.

'Ye-es,' she said through watery eyes. 'But just my dad's old car keys. And they're mine!' Huh, she really was crying now.

'Right then!' Mary said. 'They're wrong keys for a wall, er, a door, aren't they?' Brock grunted his approval, folded his wings, and sat down to watch.

I smiled, actually smiled at Fiddlesticks Milligan, and said softly, 'Go on then, try them in the snook's door.'

'I d-don't want a rotten adventure.' Fiddlesticks heaved in a deep breath, sucked up her last sob.

'Please, Wendy.'

She fiddled with her keys a bit. Rattled them half-heartedly against the back wall.

'Well?' said Fellin Tappa. 'Does it open?'

'I don't think so.' She pushed lightly against the wall. Pushed again, harder. Nothing moved.

'You've *really* got to believe the keys will turn in a lock. Got to believe a door will open. That's how it is with real magic,' I said. 'And that's what this is. Isn't it, Mary? Real magic.'

Well, Fiddlesticks just stood there confused, fresh tears beginning to leak from her face. The snook was looking anxious, and his purply-grey colour was turning a very odd yellow. 'Oh, give the flippin' things to me.' I snatched the car keys out of her hand, shut my eyes, pushed them hard against the wall, and gave one a twist.

Something clicked. 'There, see, it's a cinch!' Something creaked and groaned. Something bent, twisted and crashed to the ground with a gigantic thud. It couldn't have been a door from our house. Not even a whole wall. Nothing from our world could possibly have echoed and banged about like that. And if that sound wasn't bad enough, there was another one. Somebody was screaming. Screaming blue murder at the top of their voice . . . until a hand covered a mouth, and shut them up.

SIX

Beneath the Walls of Gorgarol

'Mmmm . . . I can't mmmm breathe.'

'Shush now, shush, girl,' the snook hissed, tightening his grip around Fiddlesticks' mouth. 'We must be as silent as spies. The door has opened upon Kacasath's domain. Our enemies could be watching us, even now. And time is running out.'

'Mmmm! But I mmmm . . . I can't breathe! And I mmmm . . . I want to go hommmme!' Somehow she wrestled her mouth free. 'I don't see why I should've been dragged along here. This silly mess has got nothing to do with me.'

'Will you be quiet, Fiddlesticks.' It was Mary's turn to hiss.

'Where are we, Fellin Tappa?' I asked, anxiously. 'What's happened to Murn? And who's this Kacasath? We still don't really know anything about anything, yet!'

'Shhhh, please – *her's* is not a name to cry

out loud. But cheer up, perhaps the weaving of your spellcraft is not all dropped stitches. For it is close to this very place that a secret meeting is to be made.' The snook gave us a funny look, and for just a moment his face lost its frown. 'We were coming here empty-handed. Without real help or hope. But now . . .' He stopped, and looked carefully about him.

'What do you mean, but now?' Fiddlesticks said. 'What does he mean, Billy?'

'I think, I think he means us.'

'Us? But I thought *they* were supposed to be *our* help. Not the other way around!'

'That's magic for you.' I shrugged, and tried to smile. But you know, I couldn't smile, not there. It was as if a terrible sorrow clung to Murn, and now it clung to me too.

I looked around me. Sometimes Murn is bright blue and gold and orange and red. Other times, when it's not feeling very well and that, it's more a kind of washed-out dirty yellowy-grey, or smudgy black. But I'd never seen it looking like this. For one thing, there was the moon. It was in the right place, up in the sky

(which you shouldn't always take for granted
in Murn) but its light seemed weak somehow,
as if its batteries were about to conk out. For
another thing, there were the mountains.
There should have been mountains everywhere, ninety-seven of them. Should have
been. But everything was wrapped up in
shadows. Vast, oily-rag shadows, one overlap-
ping the next, covering everything in turn,
until there was nothing left to see. No kind
of light was ever going to work its way
through that lot – not properly. And as for
the peculiar colour . . . there was only one –
that colour your mixing water gets at the end
of an art lesson, you know, the sludgy, soily,
purply-brown colour that hasn't really got a
name. The whole of Murn seemed to be that
colour.

'Come now, there is not far to go,' Fellin
Tappa whispered. I'd hardly noticed, but the
snook had started moving stealthily ahead of
us, was leading us forward, while the huge flying pig waddled along behind, pushing us on.
All we could do was stumble along in the middle, slipping and tripping as we went. Picking

our way as carefully as we could between scattered rocks that appeared no lighter, or darker, than the drab duskiness around us. Rocks that were crumbly dry, and coated with a chalky crust that tasted of salt.

'Billy, I want to know where we are,' Mary said.

'So do I,' Fiddlesticks said.

'So do I,' I said, pulling at Fellin Tappa's shirt sleeve. 'Where is this place? Can't you tell us where we're going?' The snook didn't stop to give me an answer. He just stopped, and we all toppled into him. Wherever we were going, it seemed we were there.

There was something ahead of us now, something vague in the shadows, standing in our way. 'It's a wall,' Mary said.

'Not a wall, a mountain,' grunted the flying pig. 'The mountain of Gorgarol.'

'Well, it looks like a wall to me.' It did. A gigantic stone wall. And it could have been a million miles high for all we could see of it. I tried looking up, but I never saw the top. The wall just disappeared into the smudgy darkness. Cautiously, I prodded the stonework with a finger. It was dry and crusty like the rocks under our feet, except its stones had been carefully cut and placed by hand, fitting snugly together.

'Well, I can't climb up there. I don't care if it's a wall or a mountain,' Fiddlesticks whined. 'I can't, so don't ask me.'

The snook was looking at us funny again. Sort of apologetically.

'What is it, Fellin Tappa?' I asked.

'This is the meeting place I spoke of, and . . . and you must wait here,' he said.

'*We* must wait here?' Mary spun herself around on her heels, as if someone was going to suddenly jump out of the shadows and go boo!

'No, not you, Mary. I, I mean I . . . There is much else to be done. Battles to be fought—'

'You don't mean you're going to leave us here!' I yelled at him.

The flying pig gave an awkward grunt and shuffled himself between me and Fellin Tappa.

'That's it, isn't it?' I said. 'That's exactly what you mean.'

Mary had been glaring at the snook, now she

was glaring at me. 'Billy, what are we going to do?'

'Well, I'm not waiting anywhere in this funny dark!' Fiddlesticks squealed. 'I'm not being kidnapped and dragged into the middle of nowhere just to be dumped.'

'For once, I think Fiddlesticks is right,' I said, surprising even myself. 'I'm not waiting here either, not until somebody tells us what this is all about.'

Brock huffed a sigh and flapped his wings uncomfortably. Fellin Tappa scowled to himself. 'There is a tale I could tell, and a warning give you. If there was time.' He stopped, shuffled about impatiently, hoping somebody was going to say, 'Oh, well, if there isn't the time, just don't bother yourself.' Well, nobody did.

In the end he settled himself down upon a rock, and began his story. 'There are some who tell the tale of a sad, tired old world, as it waits patiently for its sorry end. A world falling into eternal darkness, never-ending night. And there are some who would give this world a name, and call it Murn. And they would tell too of a Spellbinder, a spinner of life's magic, falling out of nothingness upon the face of Murn. And this magic-maker would turn the darkness into light, and the end of all things into a new beginning—'

'He's telling Murdle Clay's story,' Mary interrupted, for Fiddlesticks' benefit. 'It's not quite how I remember it, but it's our Aunt Lilly all right!' Mary gave Fiddlesticks her best, withering I-told-you-so look.

'I'm *not* finished,' said Fellin Tappa, indignantly. Then he went on regardless, with Mary and Fiddlesticks staring daggers at each other. 'There's them that say the crying rivers wept again with joy, that the ancient cities of Murn were rebuilt upon their mountaintops. That those who were lost were once more found, and that all the creatures of the dark were driven back into the shadows—' He suddenly stopped, as if to catch his breath, and looked solemnly at the flying pig. Brock gave a nod, and Fellin Tappa began again, but this time he wasn't telling old stories. This time he was talking urgently, about *now*.

'But there's them that say, and then again there's them that know. A tale is nothing but a cat's wag. One 'Binder alone is only a single stitch upon a woven cloth. Murdle Clay did her best. Bound new magic where she could. Might well have succeeded too, if it was not for, if it was not for . . .' His voice trailed off into silence. Again he looked at Brock, and sadly shook his head.

'Was not for?' I said.

Fellin Tappa was still shaking his head.

'Was not for what?' we all said together.

'Eh? Oh, for the tide coming in.'

'There it is again, tides. What tides?' Mary cried. 'Tell him, Billy. Murn's just mountains. There aren't any tides!'

'Aren't there?' Brock said, without explaining.

'An ocean's watery back is very broad,' Fellin Tappa said. 'And there's no knowing what evil wretch, what outcast of some other darker place, might not steal a ride there.'

'Like what?' I said. Not really wanting to know the answer.

'A vile creature whose very shadow is a

poison to Murn. A poison that draws other poisons to itself. And where evil brews, evil grows. Learns new ways, and greater, deadlier arts, far beyond imagining.'

'Does everybody in Murn speak double-Dutch, when they're telling stories,' interrupted Fiddlesticks, rudely. 'I can hardly understand a word he says.'

'Shush. Yes, yes they do,' I hissed. 'He just means the baddie got a lot better at being bad. That sort of thing.'

'Well, why didn't he say that?'

'*And*,' continued Fellin Tappa, in a loud, flustered voice. '*And*, as the evil one gained in strength, she named herself Kacasath of Gorgarol. Mistress of the Ninety-seven Mountains. And she brought her filthy hordes down upon the mountains, and made battle there. And the mountains of Murn began to fall to her, and numbered ninety-six. And the ninety-six mountains of Murn fell, and numbered ninety-five. And the ninety-five mountains of Murn fell, and numbered ninety-four. And the ninety-four—'

'Hang on a second.' It was me interrupting

this time. 'How many mountains does this go on for?'

'Oh, er, well, to twelve,' Fellin Tappa said, even more flustered, now. 'Yes, um, yes, to twelve I think it was. At the last count.'

'Twelve!' Mary screamed. 'Twelve mountains out of ninety-seven. Is that all that's left?'

'All that are free of *her* scourge, at the last count,' said the snook. 'Murn twelve, Kacasath of Gorgarol eighty-five.' Eighty-five, twelve! Sounded just like the rotten final score after our school rugby team's been playing a match.

'Maybe we're on the wrong side,' said Fiddlesticks. Nobody bothered to answer her.

'But what can we do?' I asked. 'If this horrible Kacasath has become so powerful not even a proper Spellbinder can stop her, we can't possibly save Murn, can we?'

The snook's face brightened a little. 'There's them that say, let those who can do. While there is a 'Binder there is a Murn. Already there are murmurings. Murn will turn again. A new thread is cast, new spells are in the making, and her friends gather at the edges of the shadows.'

'So, er, you don't really need us for anything, then? And we can go home again?' Fiddlesticks asked. 'Leave it to somebody who knows what they're doing?'

'One pair of hands is easily filled,' said Brock. ''Binder or not, Murdle Clay cannot do everything.'

'She's got that Idrik Sirk to help her with her magic.'

Fellin Tappa was looking at us in a very delicate, calculating way, now. The way my dad looks when he's after somebody to do a really rotten job for him. 'There are other tasks, greater tasks than the making of magic wars. There's them that say the last Lynth is found.'

'Last Lynth? What the heck's that?' I said.

'Well, there's them that say—'.

'Oh, never mind the "there's them that say", and just flippin' well tell us!'

'I – I don't really know,' said the snook. 'Nobody has ever seen a Lynth. It's, it's – now what might you call it? Mythical.'

'Mythical?'

'Yes, that's it. The Lynth is a mythical beast.'

'Huh,' Mary huffed. 'What isn't a mythical beast in Murn?'

'Hang on though,' I said. 'So what you're trying to say is, it doesn't exist at all. Not even in Murn!'

'Well, yes, er, or rather no. Or at least, so it was thought until—'

'And what does this Lynth do, exactly. This mythical beast that doesn't exist?'

'It holds the secrets,' said Fellin Tappa, mysteriously.

'Eh?' I said.

'It holds the secrets of every heart.'

'You mean, it sort of knows everything?' Mary asked.

'Yes,' said Fellin Tappa, with a smile. 'Sort of.'

'Everything,' Fiddlesticks said, rather guiltily. 'About everyone?'

'Yes.'

'So-o?' I said. There had to be a so-o. This had to be leading us somewhere.

'So, someone has found the last Lynth. Found it, and is waiting to tell Kacasath all about it.'

'You mean snitch, blab, and everything?'

'Snitch, and worse – is going to lead her to it. Even now she leaves the battlefields to her generals. Together, Kacasath and her snitch will hunt the Lynth to its death. And when it is dead, then she will make herself a cloak of its skin, so—'

'Urgh!' interrupted Fiddlesticks. 'That's disgusting.' I gave her a thump to shut her up.

'So? So?'

'So that she might carry its secrets upon her own back.'

'Ruddy heck,' I said.

'The greater magic would fall. The ninety-seven mountains would indeed be hers, and she their Mistress.' Fellin Tappa turned towards the flying pig, as if he needed his support. 'But even this is not the worst of it. With the Lynth would come a prize far greater than Murn alone.'

'What do you mean?' I said.

'The Lynth is the keeper of all doors.'

'Eh?'

'To everywhere,' grunted Brock, spreading

his wings wide, as if it would help explain.
'EVERYWHERE!'

'You, you mean, *everywhere*! Including our world?' I said.

Fellin Tappa and Brock nodded together.

'Flippin' ruddy Norah!'

'There's something not right here though, isn't there?' Fiddlesticks said, thoughtfully.

'Like what?' Mary said.

'Well, if this Lynth-thing knows so much about so much, then surely it knows about the plot to hunt it? All it's got to do is join up with our side. 'Spect we'd beat Kacasath easily, then.'

The pig and the snook were shuffling about uneasily. Looking at each other sort of funnily. In the next instant Fellin Tappa and Brock disappeared. Then they reappeared. Then they were gone again. Then they were back again. It was as if the money in their slot was slowly running out.

'Oh, what now?' I cried.

'And you haven't finished explaining. I'm still not sure how we're supposed to help?' Mary said.

'And you haven't answered my question!' Fiddlesticks snapped.

'Your calling spell is unwinding! It is time. We must all help in our own way.' The snook was turning a very guilty-looking red colour. 'The hunt begins and Billy and Fiddlesticks must follow after it.'

'How though? How do we do that?' I said.

'The best way you can.'

'And you just said Billy and Fiddlesticks!' cried Mary. 'What about me?'

The snook took hold of Mary's hand. 'Ah, there we have a problem. You see, there is a meeting to be made here, but only two are expected, and well – there are five of us.'

'We must go,' said the flying pig urgently. ''Binders and battles won't wait for ever.'

Mary stared at the snook. 'You want *me* to go with you?' Fellin Tappa nodded anxiously.

'No, Mary!' I yelled.

She looked at me meaningfully. 'I think I must, Billy. I'm going to help Murdle Clay and Idrik Sirk, help with their battles. You and Fiddlesticks are the spies and the hunters.'

'No, sis. If anybody should be going to a

battle it should be me!' I said.

'Oh yes. You'd do that, wouldn't you,' Fiddlesticks huffed. 'Leave two girls here, on their own. Just like a rotten boy!'

'She is right,' said Fellin Tappa. 'Each of us has their own task.'

'I don't like this. Splitting up.' I couldn't think straight.

Mary was already climbing on to the flying pig's back, behind the snook. 'Here, you'd better take these.' She unhooked the Firestone from around her neck and pulled it over Fiddlesticks' head. Then she handed me the Mamthing's jam-jar.

'Mary?'

'You're the eldest, I think you should take care of Mam now, Billy.'

'Mary, I—'

The pig, and the snook, and our Mary were all flickering now.

'I'm sorry, Billy,' Fellin Tappa shouted. 'This is the only way.'

Then . . . then they were gone.

Now that's typical of a real adventure – just when you think you're getting somewhere, finding answers, with proper help, explanations and everything – it's suddenly all gone. Taking your kid sister with it! And what's left? A horrible, shadowy, mountain of a wall, and a useless Fiddlesticks Milligan.

Huh!

SEVEN

Into the Company of Spies

'Oh, well, this is just awful. Now what are we supposed to do, Billy?' Fiddlesticks said, anxiously twiddling her hair. 'You know I can't use this Firestone-thing. I don't know why Mary gave it to me. And I'm fed up with carrying this rotten bag!' She sort of jiggled her legs about, like the bag suddenly weighed a million tons.

'Oh, stop whingeing, will you,' I snapped at her, pretending I wasn't bothered about being left on our own. 'I'll tell you what we're *supposed* to do. Just what the snook told us to do! We'll wait here for the meeting, and we'll join the hunt.'

'Well, I've said it once already. I can't climb up that wall. So just don't bother to ask me.'

'No,' I said. 'I won't.' I sat down on a rock, held the jam-jar close. Nobody was ever going to climb up that wall. We were stuck, right there, at the bottom.

How long we waited for, I couldn't say. Sometimes we dozed in fits and starts, maybe for hours, maybe just for minutes. Don't know which. But there was always the gigantic wall of Gorgarol towering ominously above us, unchanging.

We tried to have a closer look. Here and there, there were slight dips and small, shadowy hollows in its endless stone face. 'Do you think those holes are a way in?' Fiddlesticks asked. I just shrugged. What difference did it make if they were? We could never reach them. She leant backwards, held her head up, tried to see all the way to the top. 'You know, I think there's something in one of those holes.' She leant even further backwards. 'There's little knobbly bits sticking out of it.'

'Don't be daft, what knobbly bits?' I said. 'I can't see anything.' I could though, I didn't know what it was, but I could see something. 'Maybe it's a statue. Or maybe the hollows are really the poke-holes of nasty little gargoyles, with horrible, nasty little gargoyle faces that'll frighten the pants off you when they creep up on you in the dark.' It was just a joke, but I wish I hadn't bothered. I wish I'd just kept my big gob shut.

'Billy!' she hissed. 'Something's moving up there, coming out of its poke-hole.'

'Can't be.'

'It's heading this way. It must have heard you calling it names. And now it's coming to get us.' Fiddlesticks was using her best whining, wet-watery voice. 'Oh, this is worse than awful. And it's all your fault, Billy Tibbet.'

It came creeping towards us. Climbing slowly down the face of the wall, knobbly hands and feet crossing knobbly hands and feet, finding holes in the flaky stonework we couldn't even see. Getting closer. Coming nearer. Much, much nearer.

Its body was small and hunched up. Its crusty-looking skin, cracked and weather-worn. Its head was far too big for its body. Its massive ears and glaring eyes were far too big for its head. And its mouth . . . its mouth was so full up with big square teeth it took up all the room that was left on its face. 'Billy, I think we should be running—'

Too late for running. Far too late for running, now.

It was making faces at us. Horrible leering twisted-up faces. 'Urgh!' Fiddlesticks said, pulling her own kind of face. An inside-out, sucked-lemon face that was going to explode into tears. But you know, it was odd, Fiddlesticks' stupid face seemed to help, somehow.

'Hello,' the gargoyle said, cheerfully. 'Y'un made it all right'n.'

'P-p-pardon?' Fiddlesticks squeaked. But I was beginning to catch on. Pulling faces was a kind of gargoyle greeting. Like shaking hands or something. So, I pulled a face: stuck my fingers in my mouth, blew out my cheeks, and said, 'Hello.'

'My name is Grimmack. I done spied the pair o' y'un awaitin'. Now, y'un must follow me at once. No time to waste or the hunt will be on, an' we'll never catch 'em up again!' The gargoyle chuckled, and slapped his hand across his mouth. 'Oops. Shouldn't talk so loud. Could be somebody a-listenin' we don't want to hear.' He cocked his head on to one side and glanced about suspiciously. With that, he turned around and began to climb back up the wall, carefully, deliberately placing his hands and feet so that we could see where to put ours as we followed him.

Except . . . we didn't follow him. Didn't move. When at last he realised, he stopped climbing up and started climbing down again. 'This is it,' Fiddlesticks said. 'I'll bet he's not on our side at all. He'll go for us this time. You see if he doesn't.'

'Er, somethin' wrong?' Grimmack chuckled. 'Not scared o' heights, is'n?' He began scratching his huge head with his foot, as if he should be finding something useful to do while we considered his question.

'He just wants to lure us up his rotten crumbly wall. Then he'll run away and leave us dangling there, until we fall off and go splat.'

'Shut up, Fiddlesticks,' I said. 'Don't you remember anything? The kettle said friends wait in the unlikeliest places. Well, you can't get much more unlikely than this, can you?'

Luckily the gargoyle hadn't taken offence. Instead, he chuckled again and, for the second time, began to make his way back up the wall. 'Just follow me. See? It's quite safe.' This time, we did follow him. What choice did we have? 'Slowly. Hand over hand. Keep 'em eyes open, now.'

'I can't,' Fiddlesticks squeaked. 'I can't do it, Billy. I just want to go home!'

'I want you to go home! Save me having to put up with any more of your rotten whinge-ing. But you can't, so just get on with it.'

'That's it,' Grimmack chuckled. 'That's the way.'

It was a difficult, dangerous climb. And I'll admit it, I wouldn't do it again, not for – not for anything.

I remember the regular salt-dry pattern of the stones. What I could see of them, that is, with my face pressed up hard against the wall. What I could feel with my hands and feet as I clung on the best I could. I remember the wall, and I remember how every sound we made as we climbed seemed to shatter the dark silence: the gargoyle's voice, soft and low, chuckling en-couragement; the clink-clink of the Mam-thing's jam-jar, banging dangerously against the wall every time I moved; Fiddlesticks' nervous whines and snivels.

And then, another voice, hissing, answering her snivels. 'Hold on there, blessem! Keep goin'!' It wasn't an angry hiss, but calm and matter-of-fact. Like an instruction from a good teacher, one you can tell really knows what they're talking about. 'Here, take my hand, blessem.' A second gargoyle had come out of its poke-hole and was pulling Fiddlesticks' feet onto footholds, pushing her bum to get her moving upwards before she got scared stuck.

'I don't like heights,' Fiddlesticks said. 'I'm going to fall off and break my neck, I know I am.'

'Almost there, blessem.'

Another hand up, another foot. Stretching nervously for the next hold, with short, bursting breaths. A sudden slip – scraping knees and elbows against bare stone to stop yourself from falling too far. Feet waggling. Dangling dangerously over nothingness. Panicked and scared. Yes, very, very scared.

And in among it all there were stupid, niggling thoughts running around the inside of my head. Silly thoughts that wouldn't go away. What if . . . what if Fiddlesticks was right all along, what if this was a trick? What if the gargoyles were on Kacasath's side, and not ours at all? Too late to turn back, though. Nothing behind us now except empty air, pressing in around us, telling us how easy it would be to fall off.

I could tell you that as we climbed it became easier, and that we got better at it, braver, more sure of ourselves and that. Well, it didn't, and we didn't. And if I wasn't blubbering by the end of it, that was only because Fiddlesticks was doing the crying for both of us.

'Just a little further,' Grimmack chuckled. 'Hand hold to y'ur left, Billy. Stretch 'em fingers. More. Tiny bit more.'

I looked up, towards Grimmack's reassuring voice. He – he was suddenly gone. I might have panicked then, but just as suddenly, there he was again, almost right in front of me, peering cautiously out of the darkness of a poke-hole.

He tugged at my elbows, grabbed my shirt,

and I was pulled roughly upwards, and inwards. I felt my legs scrape across the sharp ridge of a stone ledge, and the sudden jolt under my feet as I discovered solid ground beneath them.

At last, *at last*, my climb was over.

My eyes were open, but it was a long time before I could see anything inside the gargoyle's poke-hole. Grimmack was waiting patiently for me to catch my breath, waiting for the others to catch us up, almost lost in a purply-blue darkness.

'In y'un go, in y'un go, blessem,' a voice hissed behind me. And the face of a reluctant, struggling Fiddlesticks appeared in the entrance to the hole.

'Ow! That was a nip! A deliberate nip! – And it's even darker in there than it is out here. How do I know this is where they went? It's probably a rotten trick.'

'Didn't we just see 'em climb in, blessem?'

'No, *we* didn't. I had my eyes closed the whole time. Urgh! And what's that horrible pong? I'm not climbing into dirty holes, full of germs and nasty diseases.'

'Come on, Fiddlesticks!' I called. 'Stop mucking about out there.'

'Is that you, Billy?'

'No, it's the flippin' bogyman. Who do you think it is!'

There was a lot more squeaking, pinching and yelping, and general argy-bargy before the two of them finally plopped over the edge and into the poke-hole.

As soon as Grimmack was satisfied everyone was safely in beside him, he simply turned around, and led the way down a narrow, low tunnel. Now gargoyles aren't very tall, so they could easily stand upright all of the way, but me and Fiddlesticks – huh – we had to crawl along on our hands and knees. Scraping off more skin, tearing clothes, snagging buttons. And the further we moved away from the shadowy opening the deeper the purply-blue darkness became. But you know, the darkness didn't seem to matter there, it wasn't frightening or anything. It was just as if the tunnels in a gargoyle's poke-hole were supposed to be very dark.

Luckily, the narrow tunnels soon opened up

into a broader space, and then into a proper cave. And surprisingly, the cave wasn't completely dark. Five or six small holes had been made in the roof, holes that must have gone all the way to the outside of the mountain because faint stabs of moonlight were shining in through them, like the tiny spotlights at the school disco. One spotlight fell on us, and one reached to the very back of the cave, to where an ancient, crumbly-looking gargoyle was sitting behind a stone table.

'Now, both o' y'un must be very quiet,' Grimmack said.

'Ahem,' coughed the gargoyle who had rescued Fiddlesticks.

Grimmack looked around, guiltily.

'Ahem,' she coughed again. 'Don't be forgettin' y'ur manners, blessem.'

'Oh, yes. Pardon me,' Grimmack chuckled. 'This'n here's Crumble. This'n here's my, er, my wife.'

Crumble politely twitched her face at me, and I politely twitched mine in return. And then Grimmack gestured towards the back of the cave. 'An' here . . . here's the eldest, an' most senior gargoyle of us all. Here's Eyesore.'

Grimmack shuffled a couple of steps closer to the ancient gargoyle, gave a low bow, twitched a rude face, and waited. Eyesore didn't seem to notice. So Grimmack shuffled forward again, ushering us with him, and pulled another face for us to copy. I stuck two fingers in my mouth, two up my nose, and sucked in my cheeks.

There was a short embarrassed silence.

'Ahem,' Crumble coughed. You see, Fiddle-sticks was just standing there, fiddling with her dress.

'Go on then,' I said.

'What?'

'Make a face.'

'I-I can't. It's just stupid.'

'Of course you can. It should be easy with a face like yours!'

'Oh, ha ha, very funny. Anyway, I think he's asleep.'

'Asleep?' Crumble said, with the beginnings of a smile. 'Why no, blessem. Gargoyles don't sleep.'

'Fiddlesticks, just make a flippin' face at him, now!'

'Oh, all right.' She half-heartedly turned up her nose and pushed out her tongue. It wasn't a very good face, but it must have meant something because the gargoyles began to chuckle, and Eyesore was suddenly startled into action.

'Eh? What? What is it? Who's there, makin' all that noise?'

'Oh, Eyesore, don't be such an old grumps,' Crumble, said, excitedly. 'These here's friends of Murn. The help Murdle Clay promised us.'

'What's that, what's that y'un say?'

'Friends o' Murn,' Grimmack yelled. 'Come to join our company o' spies.'

'Shush'n, not so loud,' Eyesore growled. 'There's some walls as has ears.'

Grimmack glanced quickly behind him, gave the cave walls his narrow-eyed, suspicious look.

'Oh, y'un worry too much, blessem! This is a big mountain,' Crumble said. 'Up's a long ways up. An' we're hidden a long, long ways down. Nobody's come a-nosin' this deep, not in many a day – what with the tides an' all. An' anyway,

don't y'un know there's a war on? With most o'
Kacasath's hordes away fightin', we've practic-
ally the whole o' Gorgarol to ourselves,
blessem!'

'Well, I still don't much like the look o' these
two,' Eyesore grumbled. 'Y'un picked up the
right pair, Grimmack? These here, look more
like . . . more like a pair o' Kacasath's *traitors*!'

'We are *not* traitors,' said Fiddlesticks.
'We're – we're Spellbinders! We've got a
proper Twitch and everything. Murdle-Lilly-
what's-her-face sent for us herself. Didn't she,
didn't she, Billy?'

Huh, I was speechless. Fiddlesticks Milligan
standing up for herself.

Grimmack and Crumble were staring at us
now. Their faces a sort of muddle between
dumbstruck awe and disbelief.

'Er, well, we're more like trainee Spellbinders, really,' I said. 'Sort of work experi-
ence. Apprentices.'

'Pah, sounds like a bladder o' hot air, to me!'
said Eyesore, shaking his head, not looking at
all impressed. 'Pah!'

Grimmack began to look very worried, as if

he really had picked us up by mistake.

'But haven't y'un forgotten somethin', husband?' Crumble asked, her face brightening with her idea. Grimmack scratched his head. 'There is an easy way o' settlin' this. Their mark. *Their mark*. That would be proof positive. I mean, y'un did ask 'em for a mark of their trade, blessem?'

'Oh dear,' Grimmack said, looking even more worried. He chuckled to himself. 'Oh dear me, no'n. I'm afraid I didn't, wife.'

'Oh, Grimmack, y'un'll be forgettin' y'ur own head next.'

'I'll be losin' my head,' he chuckled, 'if they turns out to be on *her* side.'

'Aye, aye, well, let's see 'em make their mark now, these here, so-called Spellbinders. Where's that Fiddlin'stick?' Eyesore shuffled slowly to his feet, and made his way to a gloomy corner of the cave where he rummaged among a pile of broken, rusted-up iron chests. 'Let's have Idrik Sirk's old Fiddlin'stick. A present it was, long ages since. One of a pair it is, only works in a pair, does a Fiddlin'stick. The other one's lost. Ah, here we are! Now we'll see if there's anythin' magic about 'em.'

He lifted his ancient hand to the pale light. He was holding a stick. A short stick, withered and twisted with age, and almost as thin as a pencil. As the light caught along its length I could just make out the grooves and notches that marked its surface. It had once been heavily carved, but was now rubbed almost completely smooth by endless years of worried handling.

As Grimmack and Crumble watched anxiously, Eyesore solemnly held out his Fiddlingstick towards us.

I just looked . . . and looked. Just didn't know what to do.

'Billy,' Fiddlesticks whispered, cautiously. 'Er, I think I've got an idea.'

'What?' If I'd had time to think about it properly, then I'd never have let her do what she did next. But luckily, I didn't have time to think.

She reached out and took Eyesore's stick, held it firmly between her hands. For a second she hesitated. Then, she twisted the stick between her fingers, scrunching up her face with the effort, bending it slowly in two.

'Fiddlesticks – NO!'

Bending it too far.

SNAP!

'She's broken it! Broken it clean in two!' Eyesore growled. 'I seen her do it! Seen her with my own two eyes!'

'I'm sorry. I – I thought it was a riddle, I thought, if you needed two sticks to make it work then I could, I could – Oh, here, have it back.' Fiddlesticks pushed the broken stick into Crumble's hands, and closed her fingers around it. Crumble frowned sadly, opened her fingers again and, shaking her head, began to tut-tut. She stopped, though, mid-tut, and stared at Fiddlesticks in disbelief.

'I don't believe it, blessem,' Crumble said, excitedly. 'I don't.'

'I said I was sorry, I—'

'Look, Eyesore! Look, Grimmack! The Fiddlin'stick, it's whole again. And not just one – a pair. A proper pair.'

'Can't be,' Eyesore growled.

'Can though, blessem. Can.' Crumble passed the sticks to Grimmack.

'They're even better than whole, wife,' he chuckled with delight. 'They're just like new again.' They were. The endless years of wear were gone, and in the place of a broken knobbly old stick were two small carvings: beautiful carvings, of dragons in flight.

Huh, Fiddlesticks wasn't quite so useless after all. (Of course, I didn't tell her that).

Anyway, the gargoyles had seen enough. 'See, Eyesore, see?' Grimmack chuckled out loud. 'A pair of dragons. *A pair of dragons!* Now, that's what I call a proper mark!'

'Aye, aye, maybes,' Eyesore grumbled, determined not to admit that he'd been the least bit wrong. Then he took Grimmack's carvings for himself, with the same funny look on his face my dad gets when he takes fireworks off me on Bonfire Night. (Like he was trying to pretend he was the only one responsible enough to have them, when really all he wanted was to set them off himself). 'Now we must get on. The tide might o' turned this very moment, an' the hunt will have started without us!'

'Never mind tides,' I said. 'What's the plan?'

'The plan, blessem?' Crumble said, not quite sure of herself.

'The plan?' repeated Grimmack, looking blankly at Eyesore.

'Yes,' I said. 'There's got to be a *proper* plan of action.'

'Y'un among a company o' spies now, boy,' said Eyesore, cautiously. 'So, we're goin' to join the hunt, and spy it out, o' course.'

'And then?'

'Then?'

'Yes, then? Once you've joined the hunt, once you've spied it out, what are you going to do then?'

'Pah! Stop it, o' course,' growled Eyesore. 'Stop that awful Kacasath an' her snitch from catchin' the Lynth.'

'And how – how *exactly* – are you going to do that?'

'Best ways we can, blessem,' said Crumble. 'Best ways we can.' The gargoyles looked at each other in a funny, knowing sort of way. 'An' well, we thought, that's maybes where y'un could help, what with the trainee Spell-bindin' an' all.'

'But, Billy, that's hardly a plan at all,' Fiddle-sticks cried.

I just shrugged. Eyesore was already shuffling his way out of the cave, with Crumble and Grimmack following up behind. There wasn't going to be any more awkward explaining.

EIGHT

Nightmares in the Dark

It was back to crawling behind gargoyles down their dark, stuffy little tunnels. Until the tunnels suddenly stopped, and gave way to a huge airy space. And not caves behind walls this time, but the *real* insides of the mountain of Gorgarol. 'Oh, at last, I can stand up,' I sighed. 'I thought I'd never get my legs straight again.'

'I don't think I ever will,' Fiddlesticks moaned. 'I'll be stuck, bent over double for ever.'

'Shush now, blessem,' Crumble said. 'Y'un must remember, we have left the safety o' the walls, now. Kacasath is Mistress here. Gorgarol belongs to her. This is her lair, an' the lair o' her kind.'

In the dim, shadowy light I tried to see what there was around me. It all looked as if it had once been very beautiful. There was richly carved stonework around countless arched doorways. Vast courtyards where the moonlight must once have poured through huge ceiling shafts, flooding indoor gardens. But Murn was always good at looking as if it had once been something else. And now, now it wasn't beautiful at all. Now all but one or two of the moonshafts were blocked up. Now it was just a horrible, gloomy, desolate place. And dangerous too. Stones kept running loose under our feet, or falling from walls, clattering across the floor, setting free other stones in rumbling rock falls. Or worse still, falling silently down unseen holes, with only the tiniest of sounds as they hit the ground far below.

'This mountain-castle-thingy, it's just a rotten ruin,' Fiddlesticks grumbled. 'Gives me the creeps.'

'Home to some, once upon a time,' said Grimmack, with a chuckle. 'Just be careful where y'un put y'ur feet, that's all. An' if we happens to meet anyone along the way just ignore'n. Kacasath is the only *real* bad'n. Well, an' maybes *him* too, that snitch o' hers . . . an' some o' them goblins, an' a few o' the faeries, an'—'

'Shush now, Grimmack!' Crumble demanded. 'Shush.'

The gargoyles kept moving, and we kept following. On, and on, with Grimmack always leading the way. He picked his way carefully through the dimly lit courtyards, passed the empty holes of dark, doorless doorways, that gaped at us from far-off walls. He scrambled up narrow, spiral staircases. Up more stairs than I ever want to count, or at least, up wobbly piles of rock that aimed themselves upwards as if they had once been stairs. And each time we reached the top we had to squeeze up tight to pass out on to the next level. And then, on, and on, again . . .

Every now and then Eyesore or Grimmack would call out, 'One o' theirs!' or, 'Just ignore'n,' and we'd all suddenly turn left or right as the echo of chattering voices or the clod-clod of distant feet, or the creak of a door filled the way ahead of us.

'How much further do you think it is, Billy?' Fiddlesticks whispered. 'I'm tired.'

'Oh, don't you start again.'

'I am not starting, Billy Tibbet. But I am tired. And I'm hungry!'

'Well, I don't know how far it is, do I,' I said. 'Because I don't know where we're going.' 'I don't know' is always a good answer. Gets you out of a lot of explaining. Especially when you really don't know.

Just to spite me, Fiddlesticks pulled the bag off her back and stuck her hand inside. 'You won't want this then, will you!' She pushed a squiged-up sandwich into my hand. I didn't say anything. Just took it.

'Would you like one of these, Crumble?' she asked.

'Why, whatever is it, blessem?'

'It's a sandwich. To eat.'

'To eat? Oh, I see, to eat! Well, well. No, blessem, no.' She looked at Grimmack, her face wriggling to hide a smile.

'Y'un could say as us don't really have the stomach for sand-witches.' Grimmack's face exploded into laughter.

'We're gargoyles, blessem.'

'I know that, but—'

'Gargoyles in't exactly born. They're

95

more'n . . . well, they're more *made*.'

'What?'

'Don't have the stomach for it,' Grimmack chuckled again. 'Don't have no stomach.'

'But, I don't understand, how—'

'Quiet now, quiet,' Eyesore growled softly, in a grown-up, meaningful just-don't-ask-any-more-questions kind of way. As if where gargoyles come from wasn't a very polite thing to talk about. Then he added, 'An' take warnin'. We're gettin' close, now. Close to the very top. We could easily bump into—'

'WoooooOOOOOO. WoooooOOOOOO.'

I wish his warning had come sooner.

The first moan sounded muffled, as if it was coming from the inside of a cupboard. The second moan could have come straight out of a nightmare. In fact, it did. 'WoooooOOOOOO. WoooooOOOOOO.'

Suddenly, the rotten lights went out. Just as if somebody had floated all the way up to the ceiling and covered the nearest moonshaft. (Huh, somebody had – and there wasn't another one for yonks). Everything got mixed up, then. 'Ow!' 'Where've you gone, Billy?' 'Oooh?'

'Who's that'n?' 'Get off my foot, will you!' I heard the gargoyles' feet stomp-stomping, fast as ever. But I stopped, and stood dead still, with Fiddlesticks' frightened fingers digging into my arm. Then Grimmack was yelling, somewhere up ahead of us.

'Ignore'n. It's a silly old nightmare. Just ignore'n.'

Then further away, too far away, Eyesore. 'Pah! She can't *do* nothin', she's just tryin' to scare the livin' daylights out o' y'un.'

'Well, it's working. *I am scared*,' cried Fiddlesticks, twisting up her legs, like she was bursting for the bog.

'WoooooOOOOOO. WoooooOOOOOO.' The nightmare's wail filled the darkness.

But you know, that's all it was. Woo, woo, woo. I mean, there was nothing else to it. Nobody trying to kidnap us, or lock us up inside a coffin, chop our heads off or anything. This nightmare was just a great big bag of wind. Not really scary at all. Just daft.

'Can I go home?' Fiddlesticks whined.

The nightmare tried again. Moaning and groaning, adding cackles and curses. 'Oh, go away, will you,' I snapped. 'Just go away!'

'Wooo—' The nightmare stopped, mid-woo. 'Oh well, please yourselves,' she said, sullenly. She uncovered the moonshaft, let the light back in, and let herself drift slowly down from the ceiling. She looked solid enough, but was sort of wispy at the same time. And everything about her was a dull, morbid grey. There were bits of cobwebby stringy stuff dangling from her long grey hair, and she was wearing a dreary, miserable-looking grey dress that trailed the ground even when she was floating. But you know, her face was far too young and ordinary for her to be much of a nightmare. 'Some people are no fun any more,' she said. 'Some people just don't appreciate a professional.' She didn't go away, though. She just found herself a shadow deep enough to skulk in. Every now and again trying another half-hearted sulky woo – you know, just in case.

'What do we do now, Billy?' Fiddlesticks was still clinging on to me.

'Well, we can't just stand here for ever,' I said. The gargoyles were long gone.

'Oh, I hate adventures,' Fiddlesticks whined.

'We've lost the rotten flying pig, and Fellin Tappa! Lost your rotten sister! And now we've lost the rotten gargoyles, too! We just keep losing everybody!'

'We'll find the gargoyles again,' I said, trying to sound as if I meant it.

'How?' she hissed. 'With those rotten magic stones, I suppose.'

'We might!' I said, beginning to finger my Firestone.

'Well, I won't. I just won't,' she said. 'I'll only mess it up, like I mess everything up. Can't we just keep the magic for *real* emergencies?'

'This is a *real* emergency!'

'Excuse me,' wooed the nightmare, cautiously. 'If you like, I could show you the way to the top. I know all the short cuts in Gorgarol.'

'No, thank you,' I snapped. I'd had enough of her already.

'Oh, go on. Let me. I really do know the way. I could come with you. I could help.' The woos in the nightmare's voice grew excitedly. And as she spoke, she floated out of the shadows, showering us with stringy cobwebs.

'Well, you can't come with us,' I said.

'But it's boring down here on my own.'

'No!'

'*P-lease*? Nobody *ever* wants me on their side. Not even Kacasath.'

'I wonder why?'

There was a short, huffy silence.

'I'll bet you can't guess what my name is?'

I just kept my mouth shut.

'It's Ulcerus. But you can call me Ulcie.'

'Well, *Ulcerus*, you shouldn't have scared us like that.'

'I'm sorry. I was just playing.'

'You call that playing!' Fiddlesticks cried.

'I could be on *your* side. I could. If you like?'

'NO!'

This silly argument would have gone on for ever if somebody else hadn't suddenly joined in.

'Hello. Hello. Are you receiving me?'

'Eeee!' Fiddlesticks jumped into the air like she'd been bitten on the whatsit. The voice had come from the inside of her bag.

Ulcie gave a low, worried woo, and slipped back into the shadows.

'Hello. Billy? Fiddlesticks? Can you hear

100

me? Are you there? Or are you all stone deaf?'

'Of course we can hear you,' I hissed at Fiddlesticks' bag. And then I hissed at Fiddlesticks. 'Quick, stupid, the radio!'

'Is it your aunt again? Murdle-what's-her-Lilly, the Spellbinder?'

'No. No, I think it's our Mary. In fact I'm sure. It's our Mary with a message.'

Of course, Fiddlesticks just got herself into a tizzy spin and, because the radio was at the very bottom of her bag, everything else got tipped on to the ground before she managed to pull it out.

'Mary, are you still there? Ask her if she's still there.'

Fiddlesticks gave the radio a shake, twiddled with the knobs a bit. 'Hell-o, hell-o, are you re-cei-ving us,' she said. Her voice had gone all funny and stilted, like she was trying to sound posh, or something. Huh, sounded more squeaky than the radio.

'Billy, is that you?' said the radio.

'No,' said Fiddlesticks. 'No, this is not Bil-ly. This is Wen-dy Mill-i-gan.'

'Fiddlesticks, just ask her where she is, will you!' I said.

'What is your pre-sent po-si-tion, Ma-ry?' Fiddlesticks huffed.

'I'm on Murdle Clay's mountain, Billy. I'm on the blue mountain of Escareth.'

'Are you all right Mary? Ask her if she's all right.'

'Are you all right, Ma-ry?' Fiddlesticks repeated.

'Yes, yes, of course I am. But listen, Billy—'

'And Murdle Clay? Idrik Sirk, and that?'

'Have you lo-ca-ted the Spell-bin-ders?' Fiddlesticks asked.

'Well, yes. Oh, will you just listen! It's all just too horrible, Billy! The mountain is under siege. If Escareth falls, Murn's as good as done for!'

'What?'

'Par-don, Ma-ry?'

'Kacasath's hordes are all around us. Idrik Sirk's digging in defences down on the blue plains, with the snooks and the trolls. Murdle Clay's gone to the top of the mountain to have a sit-down, and a good think about it all.'

'Par-don?'

'I'm going to lead the airforce in a counter-attack.'

'Air-force?'

'Oh, that'll be the flying pigs,' I said.

There was a sudden, juddering thud of static, a tiny plume of smoke escaped from the inside of the radio, and bits of it began dropping off.

'What's happening, Mary?'

'Oh dear. Oh no, not again!'

'Mary, what is it?' Through the radio I could hear voices in the background. Distant, unclear, scared voices.

'What? Yes. No. All right, I'm coming.'

'Mary Tibbet, will you please stop yelling yes and ruddy no! And just tell us what's happening.'

'Sorry, Billy. It's another attack. Have you found the Lynth yet?'

'Er, well no. No, not yet.'

'Sorry, I must go. Try again later, if I can.'

Without warning the radio went dead.

'Mary?' I yelled at the radio. *'Mary?'*

'Slink, plink, clink,' crackled the radio in one last feeble effort. Then, nothing more.

I quickly stuffed the bag with the bits of things I could find on the floor, and slung it on to Fiddlesticks' back. 'Come on,' I said. 'We've wasted enough time already. And where's that flippin' nightmare got herself to?'

– NINE –

The Ocean in the Sky

'I told you I knew a short cut to the top,' the nightmare wooed, excitedly.

'And about time too!' I gasped, my lungs bursting for breath. 'Seemed more like a flippin' long cut to me.' Huh, yes, I had let Ulcie show us the way. Well, after all that desperate radio stuff from our Mary, what else was I supposed to do?

Anyway, there we were, coming up the last staircase, through the last doorway and out on to the very top of the mountain of Gorgarol. Well, not quite . . .

It was sort of what I expected, and then again it wasn't. It's hard to explain. I mean, the mountain was a castle, and the castle was a mountain. It was a mountain-castle. And our doorway was at the top. It opened on to a small balcony, with steps leading down from it on all sides. The trouble was, we weren't standing at the top of a castle, and we weren't standing at the top of a mountain.

'It's a harbour, Billy,' Fiddlesticks said. 'It's a little harbour!' It was.

A deep hole had been scooped out of one side of the mountain peak, and two great walls built around its edges to make the harbour walls. There was even a gap in the middle to let the tide come in. A row of large iron rings were anchored to the tops of the walls, and here and there thick ropes had been tied and left hanging uselessly over the side. There were sets of steps too, cut into the harbour walls, one of which stopped halfway down, going nowhere, just as if the sea had really gone out. There were even bits of abandoned netting, crates and broken boxes, and the unmistakable, tantalising smell of sea salt and things fishy, clinging to the air. But the biggest giveaway of all was sitting at the very bottom of the bone-dry hole. Stranded right in the middle, was a ship. A real ship.

'That's the *Severed Head*,' Ulcie said.

'The what?'

'That's the snitch's ship, the *Severed Head*.'

'Yuk. What a horrible name.' Fiddlesticks

twisted up her face. 'And I've never seen a ship like that before.' Neither had I. The *Severed Head* was made of wood, like a proper, old-fashioned pirate ship, but it didn't look much like a proper ship. It was round, like a football cut in half. And you could only tell which bit was supposed to be the front because of the figurehead, er, figure *body* at one end (the head had been chopped off). There was no engine or anything, no oars or sails. Just a single mast with a crow's nest stuck at the top.

'And what's the point of having a harbour at the top of a mountain? An ocean can't possibly get all the way up here.'

'I don't know,' I said. 'Maybe it's a flying ship, or something.' That was just another silly guess. (And wrong).

Anyway, whatever kind of ship it was, a small crowd was gathered busily around it. In all the excitement of coming out into the harbour I hadn't even noticed them. They'd been there all the time of course, hustling and bustling all over the place, carrying and lifting, pulling things, pushing things, climbing up and down the harbour walls.

'They're loading her up for the voyage,' Ulcie said. 'For the start of the hunt.'

There must have been about thirty of them altogether, and there were all sorts of strange creatures. Some I could put names to, or at least make a good guess, like goblins and elves, hags, hexes and that. You know, all the usual sort of stupid, fairy-tale stuff. But then there were other things – things I couldn't name. The big dark things, the small flitty things, the things with no proper arms and legs that floated off the ground as if they were moving about on invisible wheels. And standing in among them all, queuing up patiently to join the crew of the *Severed Head*, were three very familiar-looking spies. Grimmack, Crumble and Eyesore.

Huh. But I instantly forgot all about spying gargoyles. Because then I saw him. *The snitch*.

He was at the seaward edge of the harbour wall – if there had been a sea – raised up on a platform of jagged rock that formed the harbour's natural end on one side. He was standing stiller than death, his head lifted up, peering out into the sky. Even from that distance, the snitch had sneak, liar, tell-tale, and dangerous, very dangerous, written all over him. And worse, I'd seen him before. At the very start, when I first touched the Firestone on the doorstep at home. He was the dark figure at the top of the dark mountain. I felt my skin prickle at the back of my neck, felt sick inside. I wanted to take hold of my Firestone, only to find myself stroking the glass of the Mam-thing's jam-jar.

'That's *him*, isn't it?' Fiddlesticks cried out. 'He's the one who's got us mixed up in all this mess. He's the one who's going to hunt down the Lynth for Kacasath. The rotten snitch!' Her voice seemed to get suddenly louder, and her words bounced around inside the harbour walls: *rotten snitch, rotten snitch, rotten snitch . . .*

'Shush, Fiddlesticks, not so ruddy loud.'

But Ulcie only wooed with laughter, and yelled out at the top of her voice, 'TELL-TALE TITCH, YOU GREAT BIG SNITCH!' Huh! Nobody took any notice. The crowd around the *Severed Head* worked busily on without a flinch, like it was an old game they'd long since grown tired of. And the snitch hadn't moved, hadn't done anything. 'See, you can call him anything you like. He can't hear you, or see you neither, for that matter.'

'But he's got eyes and ears, hasn't he?'

'Ears that refuse to listen. And eyes that, well, eyes that look only inwards – to the inside of his head.'

'Urgh, that sounds disgusting.'

'But it's not his eyes or his ears you need to worry about, it's his nose. That's what he uses to get himself about.' (Fiddlesticks was pulling faces, scrunching up her dress again). 'They say he can smell trouble a thousand miles away. He's probably smelling you at this very moment.'

'Tell her to shut up, will you, Billy.' Fiddlesticks squirmed about inside her dress. 'I'm going to be sick.'

Ulcie was wooing with laughter, again. 'I wouldn't worry though, he's got bigger fish to smell, so to speak!'

'Never mind his rotten nose,' I said. 'Who is he, Ulcie?'

'They call him Skeel. But who he really is,

nobody knows, not for sure. Some say he's the offspring of goblins and ogres. Others that he's a devil's mix – wraith and faerie.'

'But why's he doing it?' Fiddlesticks said. 'Why's he going to hunt the Lynth?'

'Why? Well, because he's on Kacasath's side, I suppose.'

'Doesn't sound like much of a reason to me,' I said.

'And he looks a bit . . . crumpled,' Fiddlesticks said. I suppose he did, from what we could see of him. He was wearing a long blood-red cloak that was wrinkled and splashed with salty-looking stains, and it hung from his skinny body in rags and tatters. There was a big hole in one side and, from underneath, part of a faded, silver-coloured tunic poked through, like the stuffing out of an old sofa.

'Has he been up there a very long time?' I asked.

'Must have been days,' Fiddlesticks said.

'Weeks more like,' Ulcie said. 'And he's never moved once since he got here. Just stands there, waiting.'

'Waiting? Waiting for what?'

'Waiting for the tide to come in, of course. Waiting for Kacasath to come in with it.'

That's all I needed to know. 'Come on then, Fiddlesticks,' I said. 'We've got to catch up with Eyesore and Grimmack.'

'What?' Fiddlesticks squeaked.

'We're going to join the crew of that ship. Do some spying of our own. Find a way to stop all of this nonsense right here.' (I didn't know exactly how, but I was). I turned to the nightmare. 'Thank you, er, Ulcie, thank you very much for your help. And, um, goodbye.'

'Couldn't I just tag along,' Ulcie wooed at me. 'As a rearguard, or something.'

'No. No, you couldn't.' I didn't have time for an argument. I tugged at Fiddlesticks' arm and started down the steps towards the harbour wall, towards the *Severed Head* and Skeel upon his jagged rock.

'Aw, go on, Billy,' Ulcie wailed, tagging along behind us anyway, in the sulks, like a youn'un who's desperate to be in your gang.

We were almost running as we clambered down the last few steps and along the top of the harbour wall itself. Skeel's platform stood directly between us and the *Severed Head*. I tried not to look at him. Tried to hurry on past.

We didn't get very far.

'What's that noise, Billy?' Fiddlesticks stopped running, and pulled me to a stop with her.

'We can't stop here!'

'There it is again.' She was looking up at the sky, with her head cocked on to one side. 'That funny faraway sound, can't you hear it?'

'That's just Ulcie in the sulks.'

'No. No, Billy, it's not.' Fiddlesticks had gone deadly serious.

Then I heard the sound too. It was distant and faint to begin with, almost like hands politely clapping at the end of a boring old speech. But loud enough to have the small crowd around the *Severed Head* charging to get on board.

'Tide's coming in!' somebody yelled. 'Tide's coming in!'

'The tide!' Ulcie wooed.

Where heavy stone doors had stood open in the mountain walls they were instantly slammed shut. Windows too. Locks were pulled, hatches closed and barred. And worried running feet were running faster.

The roar was suddenly everywhere. And not polite clapping, either – the giant yells of a football crowd, when the home team's just scored the winning goal. The roar was in the sky, on the ground, echoing across the walls of the mountain. And its centre was a huge great splodge that was already blotting out the moon.

'Oh, it's really, really here,' Ulcie wooed, squeaking with excitement. 'Quickly now, grab tight hold of something and hang on for your life!'

'What?'

There was a heavy iron ring anchored to the top of the wall, *almost* within our reach–

WHHHOOOOOOOooooooOOOOOOSSSSHHH!

The huge great splodge wasn't filling the moon any more. The huge great splodge was filling everything. The whole sky seemed to be turning slowly over. Buckling, rippling, clashing and crashing against itself. And then, whatever it was, it threw its whole weight against Gorgarol.

Wave followed wave. Real waves. You know, wet waves.

It was a sea. Bigger even – an ocean. A whole ruddy ocean, coming in on the tide all at once. Huge twists of water as big as swimming pools lashed the harbour walls. Great gulping breakers, a mile high, hurled themselves through its entrance, scooped up the *Severed Head* and threw it out upon open water.

And then, as quickly as the storm-tide had grown up, it calmed again. All in one breath, the clashing waves climbed down off the mountainsides and the harbour walls, and lay still. Its surface shimmered silvery golds, but only where the tide and the light of the moon (which had managed to poke its nose out again) were playing together at its fraying edges. The ocean had become an almost perfect mirror of water, stretching out into the sky in all directions.

'Is it safe to look yet, Billy?' Fiddlesticks said, slowly untwisting her scrunched-up face. 'Is it over?'

'Is it ever really safe to do anything in Murn?' I said, trying to straighten my fingers. My knuckles were bone-white, and agonisingly numb where I'd been clutching tight hold of the iron ring, clutching tight hold of the Mam-thing's jam-jar, too.

Fiddlesticks opened her eyes. 'Oh, just look at my dress. It's soaking wet. Soaking wet all over.'

'Oh, your dress isn't the only thing that's wet,' I said, and turned to Ulcie. 'Is it really over?'

'Not quite,' she wooed, looking anxiously out across the ocean.

'I can't see anything.' Fiddlesticks started ringing buckets of water out of her soggy dress, making puddles.

'Oh, they're on their way,' Ulcie said. 'Give them time. They're on their way.'

'They?' Fiddlesticks said. 'I don't like the sound of that.'

Below us the only movement on the water was the gentle nodding of the *Severed Head*, as it bobbed against the tide. I felt the hairs prickling at the back of my neck again. Close to the ship, a motionless figure seemed to be looking up at me out of the water. Skeel! Or at least, Skeel's reflection, as he stood upon his rocky platform, untouched by the storm.

'There's something not right about him!' I said, looking from the reflection to the real figure. But then Ulcie was wooing with excitement again.

'Look, look! Here they are. Here they come – the Sea Lords.'

'Who?'

'Kacasath's seconds. Her Sea Lords.'

Instinctively, we crouched down low; around us there were a few ships' spillings – bits of rubbish and forgotten cargo meant for the *Severed Head* – nothing proper to hide behind, but well, beggars can't be choosers.

Upon their squealing white sea horses the Sea Lords of Gorgarol came galloping across the ocean. Now, if the Sea Lords were supposed to be two of the ugliest, nastiest pieces of work Murn had ever seen – you know, to match their horrible Mistress – they didn't look much like it. They both had long silver-green hair and were wearing flashy-looking, sea-blue robes that flowed out behind them just like real waves. I don't know why they were called Sea *Lords* either, because they were women, and, I suppose, if you're interested in that kind of yukky stuff, they were beautiful and that. But a funny-looking beautiful – as cold as marble statues. They weren't carrying anything. No staffs, swords or wands, and there was nothing very wizardy or magical-looking about them. I suppose that's what proved they were the real thing. They didn't have to show off.

'Are you sure we're on the right side?' Fiddlesticks said.

'Just wait and see,' Ulcie said.

The Sea Lords galloped past the *Severed Head*, and between the harbour walls. They came to a sudden standstill beneath Skeel's rock. The sea horses stopped their squealing and fell deathly silent.

And then, out upon the horizon, where the moon flecked the ocean with its weak golds, a nasty, dirty oozing stain appeared: like an infected wound seeping poisoned blood. At that exact moment an icy coldness, as real as the shadow from a cloud blotting out a summer sun, fell across us.

'Kacasath of Gorgarol,' whispered the nightmare, and she shuddered. 'The Mistress of the Ninety-seven Mountains.'

The bleeding patch of dark sickly ooziness began to spread. And as it moved, its leaking edges drained the moonlit colours from the waters around it, until they were the same filthy stain. And so it grew, and so it came closer.

'Well, I still can't see anybody,' Fiddlesticks hissed.

'Oh, you're just not looking.'

The ooziness had reached the harbour entrance. At its heart a shadowy, haggard figure, strangely bent, and almost hidden by the disgusting yuk, came riding towards us. It was the sickliest-looking creature I'd ever seen.

'*That's* the Mistress of the Ninety-seven Mountains?' I whispered in disbelief. '*That's* Kacasath? But what is she?'

'Oh, didn't I say? She's a seaworm,' Ulcie wooed, in stricken awe.

'A what?'

'A seaworm, and the worst of them all.'

'Worms!' Fiddlesticks cried. 'Urgh, how disgusting. Nobody said anything about *worms*.'

'Looks to me like she should be stone dead,' I said. 'Only somebody forgot to bury her.'

119

'Where are you? Where are you, Skeel?'
Kacasath squealed, slithering her withered,
scaled coils between the harbour walls. There
were bits of tattered leathery cloth draped
around her neck, and tied to her thorny scales,
wherever she could get them to stay on,
making a sort of cross between a cloak and a
skirt. It looked just like peeling skin to me.

'Skeel?' she cried again. Her words seemed
to cling to the air, and left a stain behind them
that did not fade away until well after the last
echo of her voice had died. Impatiently, she
pulled herself up the harbour steps, and the
awful stink of rotting dead fish came with her.
'Do not try my patience, Master Skeel.'

Skeel had not moved, and if his nose
twitched at her stench, nobody saw. He was
waiting for her to come to him. And when she
did? Then he'd snitch everything he knew,
then he'd lead her hunt, run the Lynth to
ground, ruin Murn for ever.

Huh, but you know, just at that moment
there was something much, much worse than
all of that. You see, the only thing between
Skeel and Kacasath was *us* – us, crouched low,

desperately trying to stay hidden – and well, we'd just been spotted!

'What is this, what is this? Who would stand in *my* way?' Kacasath's voice gurgled in disbelief. Her twisted coils began to untwist, and a large, green, lopsided eye glared at me from one corner of her face. She only had the one eye – the other was closed for ever behind a thick, cruel-looking scar that made her face seem buckled.

Somehow, I forgot all about pretending to be on her side, spying things out and that. Well, I wasn't going to be scared by a crazy one-eyed monster! It couldn't be any worse than anything else we'd come across. Could it?

'I'd stand in your way! Er, I mean we, WE!' I shouted, and stood up. 'We'd stand in your rotten way. Wouldn't we, Fiddlesticks?'

'Ow, that hurt! Stop kicking me, I'm standing up, *I'm standing up*.'

'Well?' I said.

'Yes, all right. We would stand in your way!' Fiddlesticks whimpered, jumping half a step forward, just in case I tried to kick her shin again.

'Well, well. Children, little children. And human too, if I'm not mistaken. You are very far away from home,' Kacasath cackled, twisting her head towards me. 'I was warned mine was not the only heart set upon the hunting of the Lynth. But would you really run against me, child? What think you of this, my lords? Ay, Lokk? Ay, Strikken?' Below us, the Sea Lords squealed with laughter, and were forced to reign in their sea horses to hold them where they stood upon the water.

'Perhaps they do not know who you are, my lady,' called out Lord Lokk.

'Oh yes, we do,' I said. 'Oh yes, we ruddy well do!'

'And you are not frightened? Frightened out of your nasty little skins?'

'No, we're not. Are we, Fiddlesticks?'

'No,' Fiddlesticks squeaked as her voice disappeared down her throat.

'You're no Mistress of the Ninety-seven Mountains. You're just a silly seaworm.'

'It breaks my heart to hear them speak so,' lied Kacasath. 'That the minds of children are so easily poisoned, that they would play such foolish, *dangerous* games.'

'Perhaps they are not feeling so very well,' called out Lord Strikken. 'After all, what ugly-looking things they are.'

'There's nothing the matter with us!' I yelled.

I hadn't seen her move, but I'm sure the seaworm was suddenly closer to us.

'Get your Firestone ready, Fiddlesticks,' I hissed, 'and when I say now–'

I never did say now.

'WoooooooOOOOOOOOOOoooooooo. WoooooooOOOOOOOOOOoooooooo,' screamed Ulcie at the top of her voice. She had sprung out of hiding, and was floating up and down through the air, whooping and moaning, waving her arms about. Trying her very hardest to be very scary. And well, she wasn't. She wasn't scary at all.

'Enough of this tomfoolery,' Kacasath cackled. She began to slip and slide, worming her way towards us. She would have done something *really* nasty to us then, if, for the first time ever, Skeel had not moved off his stone platform, and thumped us first. We went flying, me and Fiddlesticks, tumbling head-first off the harbour wall. And Ulcie came floating after us, still wailing at the top of her voice.

'Flippin'ruddy Nor—!' I started to yell. But then I stopped again, scrunched my eyes tight shut, gritted my teeth instead. Braced myself for the splash landing!

Luckily – if there's really anything lucky about being dunked head-first into a big, wet, freezing cold ocean – luckily we could both swim, so it was a dead cinch just to plodge our way out again over the rocks below the harbour wall.

'I'll catch my death of something this time. Something really nasty,' Fiddlesticks snivelled, miserably. 'You see if I don't.'

'Don't worry,' I said. 'We're not letting Skeel get away with this.'

'Er, Billy, I think you should look behind you,' Ulcie warned, and as she spoke she drifted down behind a rock, tried to hide herself away.

As I turned around a sudden breeze rippled across the ocean. Except, there wasn't any breeze. It was the water itself, turning over, like it was having a stretch, flexing its muscles and that. The ripples grew stronger as I watched, began to churn, and became waves, lashing waves.

The rotten tide was on its way out again!

Slowly and carefully, the ocean picked itself up out of the harbour. Going out wasn't the same thing as coming in, at all. It was a much bigger fiddle-faddle altogether, with lots of lumbering about, and working up to things slowly. Like the ocean was clockwork and needed winding up to full speed ahead. It seemed to glance warily up at the moon, as if to find its bearings, and then it began to move out across the sky, wagging its great frothy white-water tails behind it. Trails of fizzing seawater dripped from the mountainsides and harbour walls, filled holes with puddles, made streams where roads had been, and a small shallow lake in the uneven surface of the harbour floor. Of course, it didn't really matter what speed the tide went out at. The ocean was still going, doing a bunk, and it was taking the *Severed Head* and the Sea Lords, taking Skeel and Kacasath, along with it.

In fact, it was taking everybody, everybody but us.

TEN

The Flight of the Kelpie

'Left behind again!' Fiddlesticks moaned. 'Oh, I wish we could just go home.'

'Listen, Fiddlesticks.' I took hold of the string around my neck, clasped the Firestone in my fist. 'You can't say it's not an emergency this time. So it's magic, or nothing!'

'Oh, bother the magic, Billy. It's not safe. And I won't get it right anyway. Prob'ly get us both killed.'

'Of course the magic's not safe. But we've got to use it, *got to*! So, start thinking.'

'What about, though?' she said.

'Anything. The Lynth.'

'Can't think about the Lynth, can I? Nobody but Skeel's ever seen it.'

'Well, a ship then, or something. While we still can. The ocean's getting away.' It was. Its watery tails were still wagging against the sides of Gorgarol, sending up great splashes of spray, still just within reach. But for how much longer?

'Oh, all right. All right, Billy, I'll do it.'
Fiddlesticks took hold of her Firestone. I heard
Ulcie's nervous wooing from behind her rock,
and then—

Bzzzz-ZZzzooonnNKK!

I hadn't noticed, but we were standing at the
edge of a shallow puddle. That's what probably
did it. First, there was a faint shimmer, the
ghost of a ripple across its surface, just as if the
echo of a distant movement had sent it flutter-
ing. Then, from somewhere *very* deep down
within that *very* shallow puddle, came a bubbling, gloopy, sloopy sound. There was a
sudden whoosh of water and the puddle
scooped itself out of the hollow it had made its
home in, and flung itself high into the air. A
billion scattered droplets of water flashed in
front of the moon – like a blazing fire of shooting stars – and then began to fall. But the
droplets of water didn't stay like shooting stars,
they didn't stay like droplets of water, either.
Two great hooves stomped the ground, raised
themselves up, stomped again, and thundered
forward. Not just hooves, but the whole of a

walloping great stallion. The horse lifted and stretched his huge head, kicked up his heels, snorting and neighing with utter delight. He was just about bursting, bursting with the joy of sudden freedom. Then he seemed to remember himself, and got all serious. He stopped jumping up and down, and stood still, and solemn.

'Don't blame me, Billy,' Fiddlesticks said. '*I* didn't think that up, and I don't like the way he's looking at us!' Neither did I.

I knew he was a horse, because he looked like a horse, but I also knew he was something very different at the same time. Ordinary horses don't come out of muddy puddles. Their bodies don't move that way either. And I don't mean his legs and head and that, like any old horse. No. His body moved even when he was standing completely still. If moved is the right word – maybe it was more like, *flowed*. Yes, his body flowed about on the inside! And as it flowed, the light of the moon glistened right through him.

'I think he's made out of glass!' Fiddlesticks said.

'No, he's not, stupid. He's ... he's a sea horse. Well, no, not a sea horse exactly, but a horse made out of the sea, made out of water from the sea.'

'He's not a horse!' the nightmare wooed. She'd had enough of hiding behind rocks and had to come poking her nose in. Couldn't help herself. 'No, he's not a horse, he's a kelpie, and—'

'Are you still here?' I interrupted. I couldn't help myself either. 'Well, you can just get yourself lost again.'

'That's gratitude for you,' Ulcie wooed, sulkily. 'I saved you all from *her*, didn't I?'

'Saved us!' I yelled. 'Saved us, my foot! All you did was mess everything up again, before we had a chance to do anything at all. Almost got us killed by that rotten Skeel.'

'I thought—'

'That's just it, you didn't think, did you?' I snapped.

'I think she's right about that kelpie though,' said Fiddlesticks, thoughtfully. 'I once read a book about one.'

'Oh yes, I'm sure you did. Just like you've

read every other book in the whole world.'

'I did. I did!'

I tried not to believe her. But I knew she was right, really. And anyway, the nightmare was nodding. The sea horse was a kelpie, and not a story-book kelpie, a real one.

'Well, I don't care what he is,' I said, determined to have the last word. 'He's still not what I asked for.'

Fiddlesticks huffed a sigh.

'Somebody must have!' Ulcie wooed.

All of this time the kelpie hadn't moved, but something about the sparkle in his eyes told me he'd been watching us, carefully. At last, he must have got fed up with waiting for us to finish our stupid argument. He lifted a hoof and ran it lazily through his puddle of water. 'Well?' he said, swaying his head slowly from me, to Ulcie, to Fiddlesticks and back again. 'Have you made up your minds?'

'Er . . . ?'

'Do you want a ride, or not?'

'A – *a ride*!' Fiddlesticks was instantly stricken.

'Why else would you have called Tarn from

beneath the waters?' The kelpie shook his mane, lowered his head into his pool, and took a drink.

'I don't know about riding, Billy. I don't think I can do it. I'm prob'ly allergic to him. I'll catch fleas. I'll fall off.'

I stopped listening to her. 'Yes! Yes, we want a ride! We've got to catch up with that.' I pointed at the ocean as it rolled slowly over, as it caught the light of the moon and winked at us. 'But, um, the tide's going out.'

Tarn lifted his head to follow my gaze, just to lower it again. 'You don't want much, do you?'

'I don't think he likes us very much,' Ulcie wooed in my ear.

I stood, silently angry, watching the kelpie. But you know, in the end, I had to trust him. What choice was there?

'We're chasing a seaworm. We're hunting the Lynth.' There I'd said it. Blabbed it straight out.

'No, Billy,' Fiddlesticks shrieked. 'We don't even know whose side he's on.'

Tarn stomped his hooves playfully in his pool and neighed with laughter. 'So, it's

Kacasath you're after, is it?' He stopped laughing and flared his nostrils at us, spraying us with seawater.

'Urgh!'

'Well, maybe it's *you* who are on *her* side! And maybe I should be turning my hooves upon you for it!'

'Maybe it doesn't matter whose side we're on,' I said. 'We called you up, so I'll bet if this is real magic stuff then you have to do what we say, anyway.' I was just guessing again, but it was worth a try. 'Or would you rather we sent you back into that muddy puddle?'

The kelpie stopped stomping, and watched the water settle in his pool. 'Ah, well spoken,' he said. He gave a long distasteful shudder, as if he'd known the answers to those questions all along.

'Oh, at last,' wooed Ulcie, bursting with excitement. 'A real adventure.'

'What do you mean? You're not coming,' I said. 'Don't even ask.' I'd had enough of arguments for one go.

'But – but I thought—'

'Well, don't think. You've done more than

enough of that already. And anyway, even if we did want you to come with us – which we don't – there isn't room.' I pointed at Tarn, who was already getting restless at our lack of going anywhere. 'There's two of us to fit on his back as it is.'

'I'm very light when I want to be,' she said, hopefully, floating gently off the ground.

The kelpie neighed anxiously. 'We must start now, while there is still a trail for me to follow.'

'Then, go. Go,' I cried. 'Come on Fiddlesticks, jump on.'

Tarn went all right, like a rocket. From a walk to a full gallop in three strides, and his hooves never once missed their footing. Each step found the next pool, or the next puddle, or the next trickling stream of water. (Always water). And then, suddenly, he went up. Up into the sky.

'Stop. Stop! I want to get off!' Fiddlesticks screamed.

'Just shut up, and keep a tight hold of his mane,' I yelled. 'I'm right here behind you!'

Tarn didn't fly, of course. Kelpies can't fly.

He just jumped nimbly on to the ocean's trailing streams of water, as if they were mountain paths to follow. He leapt furiously and, as the ocean flicked its tails and tried to shake us loose, dug in his hooves and climbed. Kept climbing until he was almost at the top, where he flung himself head-first through crashing breakers, as they tumbled from the edges of the ocean. He ran clear of them once, only to be driven back again. Cleared them twice, three times, four. Then, at last, he struggled free, and brought us out upon the ocean's gently rolling surface.

'Oh, Billy, I haven't got the stomach for sailing,' Fiddlesticks panted wheezily.

To tell you the truth, neither had I, but I couldn't say that. 'We're not sailing, we're riding a kelpie. And it's a cinch!' Wasn't though. The waves might have been rolling gently, but they didn't feel much like gently.

'I think I'm going to be seasick,' she moaned. Huh, me too! I'd gone all woozy, and what I wanted, more than anything in the whole wide world, was for the kelpie to stand still, for his body to stop rolling around underneath me.

He didn't. Tarn galloped on, jumping waves easily now, gaining speed with every stride.

'Don't look now, but we aren't alone,' he suddenly cried out.

'Where?' I said, trying to sound interested, trying not to sound very ill. 'I can't see anyone.' I couldn't. In front of us were just waves: waves glooping and sloping, curling and twisting their way across the sky.

'Behind us,' Tarn said. 'Er, on my tail, so to speak.'

Slowly, very slowly, I turned around to have a look and, as I did, I felt for the Firestone, just in case. 'Oh, it's *you* again!'

'Hello,' wooed the nightmare. She was hanging on to the kelpie's tail with both hands, flapping along behind us like a flag in the breeze.

I turned around again. Tried to ignore her. Hoped she might just go away.

'Would it help if I said I was sorry,' she wooed gently in my ear.

Something moved in my stomach. 'Where's that ruddy ship?' I shouted at the kelpie. 'We must be catching them up by now. We've been chasing them for yonks and yonks.'

'Billy!' Fiddlesticks cried. It was a Billy that left me guessing. Billy, don't be so silly. Or Billy, are you blind? Or Billy, it's right there in front of you. Anyway, I should have noticed. The kelpie was slowing down, moving forwards behind the waves now, using them for cover.

'She's over there.' The kelpie gave a nod, slowing his pace to an anxious walk.

All I could see, all I could feel inside me, was the chop and cut of endless moving water, rising and falling, rising and falling. And then, just as one wave fell, just before the next rose up again, there it was – so close to us I could read the name on its side. The *Severed Head*.

'STOP, PLEASE STOP,' I yelled out. It was the wrong thing to say. The kelpie stopped dead, almost throwing us into the ocean. And the *Severed Head* was gone from view. 'No. I mean, don't stop. I thought it looked—'

'Ye-es?'

'I thought you were going to hit them!'

'I thought catching them up was the idea?' Tarn said.

'It is!'

137

'You're sure about that? I could turn us around, take us back to Gorgarol. I mean, you do know what you're going to do when we catch them up?'

'Ummm . . .'

'More of your magic, I suppose?'

'Yes, I expect so,' I said, a bit huffily and unsure of myself. (And still feeling sick).

'Oh well, please yourself.' Tarn began to move again, but this time in a broad, sweeping circle, slowly closing in on the *Severed Head*.

'Maybe we should think this out a bit more, Billy,' Fiddlesticks said.

'Maybe you should just shut up,' I said.

Again the ship flashed into view between dipping waves. Lost again, found again. Most of the crew seemed to be on deck, leaning excitedly over the side, trying to get a better look at something in the water.

'I can't make anybody out. Not properly,' Fiddlesticks said. 'Not the gargoyles or Skeel, or—'

'Yes, you can. Look behind the ship, look who's following.'

'Urgh! It's those Sea Lords, and Kacasath!' A

disgusting, dirty trail of slime was oozing steadily into the water behind the seaworm.

'And there! See? Right at the top of the crow's nest. It's him. Skeel.'

Skeel, standing with one arm outstretched, his nose twitching, sniffing something out of the air. His arm began to move. 'He's pointing at something,' Fiddlesticks said, innocently.

'Of course he is,' Tarn said. 'He's pointing at us.'

'Well, well, well. Children. It's so *nice* to see you again.' The voice wasn't Skeel's. The voice was Kacasath's. It carried across the ocean, and seemed to fill our ears from all sides at once. Lies as sharp as dragon's teeth.

'Billy, I think you're right,' Fiddlesticks cried. 'I think it's time to try that magic stuff again.'

'Oh no!' wailed the nightmare.

'Yes, right. Right.' Huh! I couldn't think of anything really good to, er, to think of. We were on an ocean, with lots of water and that, so I just laughed and said, 'Let's do a storm. A storm would stop their rotten hunt!'

'Oh yes, Billy, yes. A storm,' Fiddlesticks said, laughing with me.

'Just keep your thinking straight, this time.'

'NO, DON'T! NOT A STORM,' Tarn cried, and he wasn't laughing. 'YOU MUSTN'T—'

Too late.

Bzzzz-ZZzzooonnNKK!

We had ourselves a storm, all right.

The air around us instantly darkened, filled up with unbroken moody-black storm clouds. Thunder growled, and a single sharp crack of blue lightning cut the sky. The ocean began to lift more heavily, swelling, rolling, tumbling. Rumbles turned to roars.

'Oh, Billy, I think we've done it wrong again!' Fiddlesticks screamed. She was right. This was a magic storm, a rotten Billy-and-Fiddlesticks magic storm, not done properly, as usual. And we'd put ourselves right in the middle of it, just where we didn't want to be. Huh, I should have known.

'Just hang on. Hang on.'

There were waves bigger than our house, bigger than mountains probably. Rising walls of water, and us, suddenly at the top, suddenly at the bottom. The waves buckled inwards, closed over our heads, became, for an instant, the walls and ceiling of a great ocean cavern, only to open up again into huge watery hands that grabbed us, and pulled us under. I choked as air and water curdled in my throat, and felt the sudden weight of the sea, its suffocating solidness. Underneath us, Tarn wriggled and squirmed, kicked out, turned, kicked out again, trying desperately to break for the surface. I heard the agonising squeal of his breath as he laboured against the strain, as he struggled to pull us to the top of the biggest wave of all. At least that's what I think the kelpie did. You see, I didn't watch. My eyes were closed, waiting to be drowned.

I didn't drown.

'I don't suppose your magic can do anything about colliding into mountains?' Tarn screeched above the roar of the storm.

'What do you mean?' I screeched back, forcing my eyes open to have a look. 'It's just another wave, isn't it?' Just distorted black shadows in the storm, playing tricks on us. Not a real mountain. Not a huge great nasty-looking mountain, standing in our way.

Huh!

ELEVEN

Miseral

'It's a wonder I wasn't drowned. Drowned to death,' Fiddlesticks moaned. That's all she'd done – moan – from the second we crashed into the mountain. 'And see, I'm so wet and cold I've gone blue all over. And there was something funny about that salt water. It's not the same as the sea at Whitley Bay. I think my skin's allergic to it. That's what skin I've got left. Just look at my knees. Prob'ly infected with something, too.'

'Huh,' I said, without even bothering to look.

The ocean had found a mountain to dump us on, had flung us ashore on its tide, done a quick shuffle to the left and disappeared around the far side. And it had taken our storm, and the whole rotten hunt, with it.

I had a quick look at the Mam-thing, took the lid off her jam-jar and poked my nose inside. She looked a bit raggy-wet and sort of limp, and there was a swimming pool swilling around in the bottom of her jar. But well, at least she was still breathing. That was enough of a look. I emptied out the water and put her lid back on (before she had the chance to snarl at me or anything).

'I wonder if there's anything left of those sandwiches?' I said to Fiddlesticks, pulling her soggy bag off her back. Then I stuck my hand inside for a rummage. 'They're a bit messy, but I think we can still eat them.'

'Urgh! I don't know how you can, Billy.'

'Easy! Got to eat,' I said, sucking the middle out of one. 'Eat, or shrivel up to nothing. Then who's going to stop Kacasath?'

'We're stuck on this stupid mountain,' Fiddlesticks said. 'How are we supposed to stop anybody? Could be here for ever and ever.'

Tarn grunted. It was the first noise the kelpie had made since we'd splash-landed. He was standing in a puddle, a very small puddle, looking very sorry for himself. Close by, Ulcie was sitting on a rock looking terribly excited and enthusiastic about something. 'This could be the right mountain,' she said. 'The *Severed*

143

Head might have been heading for here.'

'Maybe,' I said. I didn't really believe it, though. 'What we've got to do is find a way of catching them up. We don't know how long we've got left. How close Skeel is to finding the Lynth.'

'We don't really know anything,' Fiddlesticks said. 'And I'm *so* tired. I wish I could go home.'

'If you say that just once more—' I stopped myself. Threw away the rest of my soggy sandwich. 'We're shipwrecked here!' (Well, we were kelpie-wrecked really, but what the heck!) 'So we'll all just have to make the best of it, won't we?'

'But we don't even know where we are,' Fiddlesticks sulked.

Tarn looked up from his puddle. 'Miseral,' he said. 'The mountain of Miseral.'

'Sounds creepy to me,' Fiddlesticks said.

'Well, it could be worse,' I said, looking around me. It was a big, old, dreary-dark mountain, full of shadowy crags, and bent-up ugly-looking rocks. But that's all. There was nothing really odd about it, not for Murn, nothing peculiar odd, anyway.

'It could have been better,' Tarn said.

'What do you mean by that?' Fiddlesticks asked.

He didn't answer, just said, 'Now, if you've all eaten your sandwiches, we must move on. And we must move quickly.'

'Oh, goody,' Ulcie cried. She floated down off her rock and caught hold of the kelpie's tail, ready to go.

'Billy, what did Tarn mean by "could have been better"?' Fiddlesticks asked again.

I didn't answer her either. Just gave her the bag to carry, pulled myself up on to the kelpie's back, and pulled her up with me. I didn't know what he meant, and just at that moment I didn't want to find out.

'Well, maybe we should try our Firestones again, Billy?'

'Don't you dare,' Tarn warned, as he began to move. 'Don't you dare!'

At first the kelpie strode out confidently, leaping and bounding. And if he never went at his full, supersonic gallop, it was still fast enough, so I didn't worry about it. But gradually, the further we travelled, Tarn's great leaps began to shorten into long hops, and his hops into plodding, laboured steps. His hooves began to fall heavily upon the ground and dragged as he lifted them again. His shoulders sagged under our weight, and his head dropped sadly forwards. 'Stop,' I said. 'Please, stop. What's wrong with you?'

Tarn didn't stop, just said, 'We *must* keep going.'

'But what's the matter with you? Are you hurt?'

'Oh, no. Don't you see? Don't you see, Billy?' Fiddlesticks was frantic. 'It's the water!'

'What are you babbling about? What water? There isn't any water. The tide went out with the ocean, and this mountain is bone-dry.'

'Exactly, Billy! Exactly.'

The penny finally dropped. Fiddlesticks was right. Tarn was a creature of the water. He belonged to the ocean – or at least to a puddle which had once come out of the ocean. He was part of it. Only now, now . . .

I looked back the way he had brought us, to where his hooves should have cut deep grooves in the dry earth. Behind us stretched an endless line of tiny hoof-shaped puddles. As if the kelpie was leaking. As if the water inside of him was slowly draining away. As if *he* was draining away.

'Stop,' I yelled. 'I-I command you to stop. And I really do mean it this time. STOP.'

'There are dangers all around us,' said Tarn, wearily. 'This is Miseral! They may be unseen as yet, but they are there, none the less.'

I wasn't going to argue any more about it. If he wasn't going to stop on his own, I'd make him stop. I pushed Fiddlesticks off his back, and threw myself after her.

'Ooowww!' There were screams and yells and tantrums then, all right. Tarn reared up on his hind legs, fretting and stomping, wildly shaking his mane. With a flick of his tail, he tossed Ulcie to the ground. Then he grabbed for my shirt with his teeth, and tried to pull me up, tried to force me to climb back on to him.

'I won't,' I said bluntly, ripping my shirt free. 'I won't. Not until we've done something to help you. Will we, Fiddlesticks?'

Fiddlesticks just groaned. 'I think you've broken my neck.'

147

'We must not stop here. Not here,' Tarn cried anxiously. 'We have stayed on this mountain too long already.'

'But there's nothing here to worry about,' I said. 'Just a few silly rocks and—'

Something moved.

Something among the rocks moved.

Ulcie picked herself up, gave a sudden shivery woo, and ran and hid behind the kelpie.

There were no shadows for something to hide in. Not proper nasty scary ones. But that just made it all worse somehow.

'What was that!' Fiddlesticks squeaked. The something among the rocks moved again, but behind me this time. Then I felt the icy cold. The bitter, icy cold climbing up my back. And a murky shroud of mist slipped quietly in around our feet.

'Who – who's there?' I said, making my voice loud, as loud as the tightening in my throat would let it go, pretending I was brave. 'Come on out. You don't scare us with your silly games.' They did though. And their answer was silence, and another movement, further away this time, but edging forward. The kelpie's teeth were digging into my shoulder again.

'Billy, I don't like this,' Fiddlesticks mouthed, too frightened even to whisper.

I was almost turning around, turning to climb on to the kelpie's back. Almost ready to make a desperate dash for it, even if it meant leaving Fiddlesticks and Ulcie behind. That was, until I looked at the kelpie. Tarn was so weak, so feeble now, he could hardly hold himself upright. He could never carry us. Not even one of us.

Then came the murmuring. The silent murmuring. That's all I can call it. It was as if the silence of the mountain was talking to us, whispering, poisoning us with words that were there but couldn't be heard. And I knew, just knew that they – whatever they were – were all around us now.

'Lurkers,' Tarn whispered, in a voice that was so very low and distant, it seemed to come from the far side of another world. 'I did warn you. This *is* the mountain of Miseral.'

'But what's lurkers?' I asked, not really wanting to know the answer.

'Lurkers? They are the creepy back lane that no one dares to venture down. They are the single lonely tree on an empty hillside that must be shied away from. They are the dark cracks in the pavement where you must not put your feet. They are the unexplained, the fleeting shadow across an empty wall. Never there. Always there.'

'Oh well, that's cheered me up a whole heap,' Fiddlesticks said.

'Get your Firestone ready,' I said.

The kelpie reared up, wildly shaking his head.

'I don't care,' I said. 'Anything's got to be better than this horrible mess.'

We should have thought it through a bit. Worked it all out properly. Planned exactly what it was we wanted. Well, we didn't, did we? We just grabbed hold of our Firestones and ...

Bzzzz-ZZzzooonnNKK!

The biting cold was instantly roasting hot, and a blinding white light smothered the mountain's purply-blue drabness. 'Oh no, what's happened this time?' I could hardly bring myself to look.

'It's like . . . it's like the sun, Billy. A tiny little sun.'

'There isn't any sun in Murn.'

'Well, there is now. There is now.'

Of all the really stupid things to conjure up we'd made a . . . well, we'd made a sunny spell. But you know, however silly it might have seemed, it was working.

The lurkers were suddenly gone.

'Oh, Billy, it feels so wonderful.' The tingling warmth from that tiny little sun spread inside me, like a mug of boiling hot milk on a freezing cold winter's night. Where our clothes had clung sticky-wet to our skin, now they were dry. I held the Mam-thing's jam-jar up to the sun. Watched her soggy fur fluff instantly dry, watched her squirm with delight, and we all started to laugh. That is . . . all of us, except Tarn.

'Oh no. OH NO!' I might have guessed something would go wrong with our spell. There was steam coming out of him, a bit like the stuff you get off a puddle when it's about to evaporate. In fact, exactly like the steam you get when a puddle dries up. The kelpie was disappearing right there in front of us. The heat from our sun was turning him into a steamy, wispy nothingness.

'Billy! Do something. You've got to *do* something.' Fiddlesticks and Ulcie were jumping up and down on the spot.

'Well, don't just stand there having ruddy hysterics. The Firestone!'

But there wasn't time. Tarn was gone. Gone.

'Oh, Billy, *Billy* . . .' Fiddlesticks looked desperately from Ulcie to me. Nothing helped. I felt the sting of a tear prick my eyes, but I fought it back, fought it back like mad.

You see, the kelpie wasn't the last thing to vanish. The sun was already getting less sunny. Our sunny spell was almost over. And as the sun went, the icy coldness and the fear came back. As the sun went, the purply-blue drabness came back. As the sun went, the lurkers came back. All of them. All at once. All around us. And their mists came with them.

No time to run, to call out to Fiddlesticks or Ulcie, to feel for a safe hand—

'Over here. This way,' a voice suddenly

bellowed, somewhere out in the murkiness. A booming, roaring voice, that was trying really hard to be a soft whisper, and failing miserably. As it spoke a howling gale rushed past us, almost knocking us off our feet.

'Urgh! What's that horrible stink?' Fiddlesticks whined.

'Who – who's out there?' I called.

'It'll be a trick, Billy,' Fiddlesticks said. 'Those horrible lurkers, trying to lure us away.'

The last of our sun plinked out, like a light bulb breaking.

'Quickly now. This way!' Another booming whisper. Another howling gale, and a rotten stink.

I don't know what it was that made me move. There was something in that voice, something that told me its owner was much bigger, much stronger, and much *much* more dangerous than the lurkers could ever be. And yet . . . I took a step towards it, through the mists.

The lurkers had fallen back, taken to lurking just close enough to keep an eye on us, but far enough away to make a run for it, should the owner of the voice decide to do something. In a strange way, I was glad our sunny spell had gone. There are some places I think it's best the light doesn't go poking its nose. Some things are better left alone.

I took another half-step towards the voice.

Ulcie wooed nervously.

'Billy, be careful,' Fiddlesticks said, and she hesitated. And I hesitated too – until the voice called to me again.

'I won't hurt you. This way. That's it. That's right.'

'Come on, Ulcie. Fiddlesticks! Come on!'

'Oh, all right. But I hate adventures. I do. I really, really do.'

With the lurkers' mist lying so heavily upon the ground we couldn't see a thing, but we kept walking anyway. We followed the voice as it called to us, followed the noises too – the heavy juddering thuds that sounded like a very big pair of feet clomp-clomping their way ahead of us – just happy that the lurkers weren't leaping out at us.

The clomp-clomping stopped. We hadn't gone far.

'Step up, please,' boomed the voice. 'Just ahead of you. That's it, that's right.'

'I can't see any step,' Fiddlesticks hissed.

'Yes. Yes, there it is. Just in front of us,' wooed Ulcie. 'It's a rock or something.'

'It doesn't feel like rock, Billy. It feels more like leather, or, or skin!'

'Oh, don't be so daft.'

'Are you all safely on?' boomed the voice.

'Yes, but—'

WHhhhoooooooosssSHHH!

Our step shot up into the air, like the express lift in Woolworths gone mad. If we had been at the bottom of a misty mountain, we weren't now. Now, we were very definitely at the top. And there was moonlight, and sky and fresh air, and oh, everything.

'Where – where is it, then?' Fiddlesticks gasped, trying to catch her breath. 'The *thing*, the thing with the voice.'

'Hello,' I called out. 'Where are you?' For a moment there was no answer. Just a long, thoughtful silence, like somebody was having a very serious think.

'Er, I'm here,' the voice said, cautiously. The

rush of air almost toppled us off our step, would have blown Ulcie clean away if I hadn't made a grab for her as she flew past.

We weren't standing on a step at all. It wasn't a step, or a rock, or Woolworths' lift. Wasn't the top of a mountain either. *It was a hand!* And from behind the hand we were being watched by a pair of very large, very curious, jet-black eyes.

'Oh, Billy!' Fiddlesticks whimpered.

'Flippin' heck. Flippin' ruddy heck. It's a great big—'

'Giant!' Ulcie wooed, with a very odd mixture of panic and professional admiration in her voice.

'That's it. That's right. My name's Ogrin,' said the giant. 'Ogrin Thug.' Then he giggled, as if his name was really funny, and almost juggled us out of his hand.

'Oh, Billy!' Fiddlesticks whimpered again. 'And doesn't he ever clean his teeth? If he keeps breathing on me with that disgusting breath, I'll be sick. I know I will.'

'Oh, for goodness sake, stop squeaking,' I said. 'You'll scare him.'

'Scare him. Scare *him*. He's prob'ly going to eat us. Prob'ly going to snap us up into tiny little bits—'

'Will you shut up,' I hissed, and somehow managed to close my hand over Fiddlesticks' mouth, before she could say anything else.

'My name's Ulcerus,' the nightmare said, as loudly as she could, drowning out the last of Fiddlesticks' protests. 'Of course, all my friends call me Ulcie. This here, is Billy. And this . . . and this . . .' She hesitated as I tried to get a firmer grip on Fiddlesticks' mouth. 'You'll have to excuse our friend, she's not really feeling very well.'

The giant shuffled his feet, and pushed his enormous face closer to us. 'You don't want to go messing around with lurkers. It's not safe.'

'We got ourselves a bit lost,' I said. 'We're trying to find someone—' Ogrin wasn't listening.

'Got to stomp on 'em. That's it, that's right.'

'We're TRYING to FIND someone,' I said again, in a louder voice. The way my dad talks when he's asking directions from the locals on one of his Spanish Super Summer Saver holidays. 'I WONDERED, IF MAYBE you could HELP US?' He still wasn't listening.

'No, little 'uns can't go messing with the likes of 'em. Give 'em a good stomping! That's what I says.'

Fiddlesticks struggled to get her mouth free. 'Is he deaf, or something,' she squealed. 'Are you deaf – Woooooaaa!'

We were suddenly on the move again. The giant lolloping and stomping. And some of his stomping sounded just like snapping and cracking, and grinding up.

'I wonder what he's walking on?' I said.

Ulcie wooed. But if she knew, she wasn't going to say.

'Ogrin will help. Take you to Aul'Jewen. That's it, that's right,' said the giant. 'Ogrin will take you to the four mountains of Aul'Jewen. Ogrin Thug seen it all. Seen everything from the top of his mountain, did Ogrin.'

I tried desperately not to look down. Not until Ogrin stopped lolloping and stood still. Not until my hand slipped from Fiddlesticks' mouth and she started screaming blue murder.

Ogrin was standing on the very edge of the

mountain: the very edge, of the very edge of Miseral. In front of us was . . . nothing. Not a great big going-on-for-ever nothing. More a football-pitch-with-a-playground-next-to-it-sized nothing. Beyond I could see three mountains.

'Them's Aul'Jewen,' said Ogrin.

'I thought you said four—' But before I could have a proper look, he spun himself around to face the other way.

'First though, I want to show you something else.'

– TWELVE –

The Battle of Escareth

In front of us now was – well, another nothing. But this time it was just nothing, a purply-black nothing. 'What are we supposed to be looking at?' Fiddlesticks whispered, twiddling idly with her hair.

'I don't know.'

'Oh, they'll be at it again, soon enough,' the giant grunted disapprovingly, and began to sigh, like he was watching something really really sad on the telly.

'Billy,' Fiddlesticks hissed, 'I still can't see anything.'

'Neither can I!'

The giant tut-tutted, in a sad knowing sort of way, as if, whatever it was he was watching, he'd seen it all before, a thousand times. 'Sees everything from his mountain-top, does Ogrin,' he said.

'Well, I ruddy well wish I could see everything,' I said. For once, Fiddlesticks and me had the same idea, and together we grabbed for our Firestones.

That was the strangest *Bzzzz-ZZzzooonn-NKK!* of them all. Nothing much happened. The darkness around us didn't disappear or anything. Neither did we. It's a bit difficult to explain. I began to see right through the darkness, right through it, for ever and ever and that, like my eyes had turned into a gigantic pair of binoculars.

'Eeeee!' Fiddlesticks cried. 'Can you see that, Billy?'

'Yes. Yes I can.'

A flash of blue streaked across the purply-blackness, burst into a whole rainbow of crackling, sparkling colours, filled the sky, lit up the tops of distant mountains that had been hidden there.

We kept looking.

It went quiet again after that, but the glow around the mountains stayed a fuzzy silvery-grey. 'Look closer,' said the giant. 'And see what Ogrin Thug sees.'

A single mountain-top stood clear of all the rest. A bright blue mountain. *Escareth!*

'I can see more. I can see, I can see – Billy, it's a battle!' Fiddlesticks squealed. 'Urgh, I don't think I can watch.' She scrunched up her face until her eyes were nearly closed. Would have turned away too, if I'd let her.

'Don't you dare, you'll break the spell!' And if I bullied her, well, I had to. Didn't I?

It was a battle. A battle at its very height. There were Kacasath's hordes – you know, the goblins and the hags, the dark nameless flitty things and that. Even without their Mistress they surged across the blue plains of Escareth, falling upon the stricken defenders. On and on they came in never-ending lines. More, and more, and still more. And it was not a special magic power or a sense of purpose that carried them forwards, just the weight of their numbers. Huh, sometimes numbers are enough. Like when you're playing hundred-a-side football in the yard at school. Best players don't get a look-in, it's just the biggest team that wins.

I focused in with my binocular eyes. There, at one end of the battlefield, was Idrik Sirk, and at the other Murdle Clay – the Spellbinders of Murn – wielding spells for all they were worth.

Cutting great holes in the advancing armies.

Didn't stop them though. On they came, yet more and more again.

Then I saw the beautiful dragons of Murn. Dragons sworn never to lift their claws against any enemy, because . . . well, because they just wouldn't. I saw them standing there, simply putting their huge bodies between the defenders and the swarming hordes. I saw them fall, one by one, as the mass surged over them, and even from all those miles away I heard the mocking cackles, the roar of dragon fire, the horrible, bitter cries of death.

And then, and then . . . I saw the sky filling up again, but with pigs this time. Flying pigs. It was our Mary's airforce! And there was Mary, riding on the back of Brock, sweeping down through the air screaming her ruddy head off. Urging her pigs on.

'Go on, Mary!' I yelled. 'Go on, sis, get stuck in there!'

She did. She ruddy well did, and for a moment the hordes fell back in disarray. Fiddlesticks and me were suddenly laughing like idiots with tears streaming down our faces. And beside me

Ulcie and the Mam-thing in her jam-jar joined in, even though they couldn't see a thing.

The 'Binders took their chance, hurled their best stuff at the hordes in one great big dollop. Cut the advancing armies clean in two.

Huh, but *still* they came on . . .

'Oh, Billy,' Fiddlesticks snivelled through her tears. 'I want to help. I want to help your Mary win.'

'She's a thousand ruddy miles away!' I turned and stared up at Ogrin, but the giant only shook his head sadly. 'Oh, come on, Mary,' I screamed in frustration, puffing and blowing with anger. I was still holding the Firestone and it was still warm with the heat of our spell.

And you know what? Something peculiar happened then. Around us a wind began to whip up and roar. Worked itself up from soft puffing breaths, into a raging storm.

Far away, out upon the battlefield, I could still see Mary and Brock. As I watched them, as I puffed and blew, the slightest tickle of a breeze caught in Mary's hair, rippled the feathers of the flying pig's wings.

'That's it, Fiddlesticks! That's the answer!'

'What is, Billy? What? Oh, I wish *I* could see!' wooed Ulcie.

'Fiddlesticks, start blowing!'

'Eh?'

'*Blowing!* Just do it, will you. And keep it going, control it. It's got to go to exactly the right spot.'

We filled our lungs, filled them until we were bursting bright red – then we blew all right. Blew our flippin' guts out. Raging storms became a roaring hurricane with twirling whirlwinds and everything.

Our roaring breath hit the hordes smack on. Swept them off their feet, sent them reeling good and proper.

'Yes!' squealed Fiddlesticks, with delight. 'Yes! Yes! We did it, didn't we, Billy? We did it right!' I just laughed, laughed with her.

That's when the *real* fightback started! Mary and the flying pigs were already making ground. The 'Binders too – the air was bright blue with new magic. At last, something was turning Murn's way. And with Kacasath out of the way, chasing after Lynths and that, Murn might even win!

But the battle of Escareth wasn't the only thing that was turning.

Ogrin Thug was on the move again. All of this time, we had been watching the battle from the very top of his mountain, and well, he'd seen enough.

'Billy, will Mary be all right? I mean, I mean . . . she won't be hurt or, or dead or anything, will she?' The giant didn't let me answer, even if I could have done. He was spinning around on his heels again, breaking our spell. Behind us Escareth was lost again to the darkness, and in front of us now, beyond a gaping nothingness, towered the mountains of Aul'Jewen.

THIRTEEN

'Pssssssssssst. Pssssssssssst.'

The three mountains of Aul'Jewen were bent and twisted like corkscrews. (If there was a fourth mountain, I couldn't see it). The top of the first mountain had been snapped clean off and was lying on its side at the bottom of the third mountain. The second mountain was leaning awkwardly, in a very unbalanced sort of way, and rested uneasily against the other two for support. But whatever was wrong with those mountains, whatever had happened there, had happened a very long time ago: ancient history, I think it's called. I was more worried about *now*. You see, the lump of nothing between us and Aul'Jewen was getting worryingly narrow.

Ogrin had jumped off the mountain edge.

'Aaaaarrrgh!' Fiddlesticks and me screamed together. Nobody could possibly jump that gap. Not even a giant four times as big as a double-decker bus.

'Weeeeeeeeee!' Ulcie cried.

Ogrin cleared the gap . . . nearly.

His outstretched arms flapped wildly, flapping us wildly at the end of them, as he began to fall. His free hand made a desperate grab for something, for anything, and found nothing. His fingers slipped through thin air, clutched for a moment at solidness, took a hold there, lost it again, and began to slide sickeningly downwards—

'Got it!' he cried, sighing with relief. We juddered to a halt as his foot caught on something firm. 'That's it. That's right.' He began to raise himself up again on one arm. Then he swung his legs up after him, and scrambled to his feet.

'Aul'Jewen,' he laughed. 'Ogrin knew he could do it.' (I'm glad somebody did!) He didn't wait to catch his breath, or say he was sorry. He was off again, lolloping at full pelt. He cleared the top of the first corkscrew mountain in less than a dozen strides. Tiptoed gingerly across the second, and only burst out laughing when the whole thing suddenly creaked and groaned as it took his full weight. When, at last, he did stop, we had cleared the top of the third mountain, and were safely down its far side.

Ogrin stood perfectly still, and listened carefully. Only when he was absolutely sure we were on our own, which took an awfully long time, did he speak. 'That's it. That's right. That's what you'll be looking for. Ogrin sees it. Sees everything, does Ogrin, from the top of his mountain.' He started to laugh, but then thought better of it. Instead he shook his head, and sighed sadly, smothering us with another warm blast of his smelly stale breath. With his free hand, the one that wasn't holding on to us, he pointed to the ground.

To be honest, I was feeling rotten after all the jiggling up and down across mountains and stuff, so I didn't really take in much of what he wanted us to look at. We were standing in a shallow valley – I did notice that – a valley sandwiched between the third mountain of Aul'Jewen and the small bump of a hill that was only just taller than the giant himself. In the valley bottom, there were funny, dark bits of *something*, scattered like litter along its whole length.

Ogrin took a step towards the small hill,

stood up on tiptoes, and peered cautiously over the top. 'There's the fourth mountain of Aul'Jewen,' he said.

'Behind that hill?' I said. The giant nodded.

'It can't be much of a mountain if it's smaller than a hill,' Fiddlesticks said. Luckily Ogrin didn't seem to hear her.

'This is where they, um, where they came aground. In this here valley, amid the ocean storm. Them's you're chasing after, that is.' He hesitated and gave us a curious look – as if he was warning us he knew everything about everything we were doing, even though we hadn't told him a thing. 'And yon's the way he took them, the snitch. Yon's the way for you to follow, now. Across the fourth mountain.'

'But you're coming with us,' Fiddlesticks demanded. 'Aren't you? Billy? Isn't he? Isn't he coming with us?'

The giant scratched his huge head. Then simply lowered himself down on to one knee, and gently placed us on the ground.

'Ogrin is hungry now,' he grumbled.

'What?' I asked vaguely.

'You see, he is going to eat us. I knew it.

Knew it all along,' Fiddlesticks whimpered, screwing up the bottom of her dress until she'd nearly pulled it over her head. 'Scaring us half to death, running us up and down mountains. And now he's going to eat us!'

Ogrin scratched his head again, and stood up, muttering softly to himself. Then he belched, very loudly, and sent rocks tumbling from the sides of the mountains. 'O-oops! Sorry. Too many lurkers for dinner.' He shook his head and rubbed his stomach. '*Always* lurkers for dinner.' And with that he leapt forward. Three stomping steps, a short leap, and he disappeared over the top of the third mountain. Disappeared without even a glance back over his shoulder.

'Hang on!' I yelled after him. 'Don't go yet. How do we . . . how do we . . .'

Ogrin Thug was gone. He didn't even say goodbye.

'I'll bet he could have helped us if he'd really wanted to,' Fiddlesticks huffed. 'I mean, he could have done some proper stomping for a start. Skeel, and those rotten Sea Lords. Or *her*, that rotten Kacasath-worm-thingy. He could at

171

least have stomped on her for us. That's if he really was on our side.'

'I think he has helped us, in his own way,' I said, looking at Ulcie. She seemed to avoid my glance, and played innocently with the cobwebs in her hair.

'Well, giants aren't really on anybody's side, are they?' she said. 'Don't have to be.'

It was only then that I began to look around me properly, began to see exactly where Ogrin had left us. There were bits of wood – torn, splintered, chewed-up bits of wood – scattered wildly everywhere. And here and there, slimy, snaky, oily-rag stains: the disgusting trailings of a seaworm.

'Billy, Ulcie, what's that over there, sticking out of the ground?' Fiddlesticks had turned a very odd shade of green. 'It's got no head!'

I forced myself to look. 'Stupid! Stupid! Why didn't I see?' I clonked myself on the head. 'It's the *Severed Head*. This is the wreck of Skeel's ship. And that's the mascot. Just the mascot-thing. It's not real!'

'But if it's not real, Billy, why is it bleeding?'

'Urgh!' Ulcie wooed, like she was trying to

stop herself from being sick. 'I was never one for the blood and guts end of the trade!' Then she fainted. Fell over in a heap.

'No, it can't be blood,' I said. 'Can't be.'

Was though.

You see, it wasn't *just* a wrecked ship. No. Ships have crews. And I know they were our enemy – the goblins, and the hags, the nameless flitty things and that – but to see them drowned, their bodies broken and twisted up like stringless puppets by the anger of the storm—

Anyway, it was just about then that somebody else tried to attract my attention.

'Psssssssssst. Psssssssssst.'

'Eh? What?' Horrible, cold needles of sweat prickled me all over.

'Psssssssssst. Psssssssssst,' the Psssssssssst said again. Just behind me, a big, upside-down lump of the wrecked ship had come to rest. I was sure the muffled Psssssssssst was coming from there.

A very fragile-looking nightmare lifted herself unsteadily from the ground, and floated behind me, put me neatly between the Psssssssssst and herself. Fiddlesticks too had moved close, and was twisting her legs, fiddling with the bottom of her dress. I took hold of her hand to, to— Well, I just did, that's all.

'Psssssssssst, is it safe to come out yet? Is it safe?' said the Psssssssssst.

'You'd better come out. Whoever you are. I – we – we're Spellbinders. And there's hundreds of us,' I lied in the biggest voice I could find. 'And we won't stand for any silly nonsense.'

'All right'n.' The wreck began to shift and slide about, creaking and tearing apart from the inside out. And there, right in front of us, stood Grimmack, the gargoyle.

'Oh, it's only *you*. You almost scared us to ruddy – scared us to ruddy–' I'd meant to give him a right earful, but I didn't, or rather, I couldn't. You see, it wasn't just Grimmack, it was Crumble too, and they were both very badly chipped and cracked all over – as if a rotten vandal had been bashing them with an iron bar. One of Crumble's ears and the end of her nose had been snapped off. But poor Grimmack had taken the worst of it. There was

174

a very nasty green stain splashed all over him, and his left arm was completely missing below the elbow. I didn't do any more shouting. Instead I pretended not to notice the horrible mess they were in, and pulled the nastiest face I could think of. Poked Fiddlesticks in the back, until she did the same.

Grimmack sort of half-chuckled, and pulled his worst face back at us.

'Oh, it's so good to see you,' Fiddlesticks said. And then she couldn't pretend any longer, and tears flooded her face. There were all sorts of hellos and sorrys then, handshakes, hugs, stupid cuddles and that. You know, private stuff.

'But what . . . what on earth happened?' I said at last, as Fiddlesticks and Crumble wiped away the last of their tears.

'It were terrible, blessem,' Crumble said, sadly. 'It were us spies. We done scuttled her, the *Severed Head*. We sunk her.'

'Sunk her? But how?'

'We'd been posted below decks, blessem. Aye, deep down in her belly.'

'But we still gets ourselves a sneak look at

y'ur magic storm, Billy,' added Grimmack, with a chuckle.

'Aye, that old ship were so full o' holes to peek through it were a wonder she didn't sink herself, blessem! Anyway,' she continued with their story, 'we thought as how it were as good a time as any to make our move against Skeel. Us bein' the spies'n all. An' well, it were Eyesore's idea, blessem. His old eyes just comes alight with it, an' he pulls somethin' from his belt. Somethin' he'd carried there ever since leavin' his poke-hole – the Fiddlin'sticks! "What y'un think these is for?" he says. Then he holds 'em up, an' starts his fiddlin'.

'Weren't just sticks then, they weren't just carved wood in a dragon's form. No, not when y'un's got yourself a proper pair o' Fiddlin'- sticks, made by a 'Binder's hand. They were *real* dragons. Real dragons! With flames, an' claws, an' wings an' everythin'.

'Well, that old ship's rotten planks done split apart, what with the dragons' size, and weight, and everythin'.'

'Crackety, crackety it went,' Grimmack chuckled.

'Aye, crackety, crackety plosh!' Crumble finished. 'In comes the water, glug, glug, glug. Out goes the dragons, an' they takes poor Eyesore with 'em.'

'Then there were panic aboard! Aye, the whole o' Skeel's crew screamin' an' yellin',' Grimmack said. 'An' nobody's tryin' to plug the hole where the water's pourin' in, until it's far too late to save her.'

'But I still don't understand,' I said. 'If the ship was sinking, how did you all get here?'

The gargoyles fell silent, as they remembered. 'That were *him*,' Grimmack said, quietly. 'That were Skeel. He done turned the *Severed Head* for the shore, by some tricky spellcraft o' his own makin'. Kept her afloat through the height o' the storm, an' long after she should have gone under, by rights. Long, long after.'

'But what about poor Eyesore? What happened to him?' Fiddlesticks asked, anxiously.

No chuckles now. Grimmack and Crumble looked sadly at each other, and then at us. Their silly faces not silly any more, but suddenly old and drawn, and tired, very tired.

'Oh,' I said. Just 'oh'. I wanted to say a lot more. Something that would help. But there wasn't anything that would help. So I just said 'oh'.

There was an odd, uncomfortable silence then. A silence that was very difficult to break. Finally, it was Ulcie who wooed softly, and asked, 'What about Skeel? What about the snitch and his Mistress – Kacasath?'

'Well,' Grimmack said. 'Well, when the *Severed Head* finally comes aground amid the storm, she were all smashed an' broken. Them o' the crew as could find a way, struggled ashore. Them as couldn't, an' that were many, followed the dragons to the oceans' depths or, or . . .' Grimmack hesitated, stroked the end of his broken arm, thoughtfully, looked sadly about him. 'O' course that Kacasath came chargin' ashore after us, all fired up by the magic o' the storm. She were furious. 'Specially as her Sea Lords had strangely gone amiss among it all, an' have never been seen since.'

'Aye, we thought it were the end for us all, blessem,' Crumble said. 'Would have been too, if that Skeel hadn't have stepped right up an' said as how, just by chance, this were the exact place he'd been on the look-out for all along. An' how there were no more time for arguin', an' that there were a hunt to be finished.'

'You mean, you shipwrecked the *Severed Head* just where they wanted to be, anyway! What rotten use is that to anybody!' Fiddlesticks was bursting.

The gargoyles looked away, guiltily.

'Well, at least they tried,' I said, ready to thump her. 'Can't blame Eyeso—, can't blame anyone for that. And anyway, we're stuck with it. Ogrin showed us the way to go. So we'd better just get after them.'

Crumble gave me her best grimaced face, tried to cheer us all up a bit. So I stuck my fingers in my mouth and screwed up my face back at her. 'Yes, blessem,' she said, softly. 'I think we'd best had, but . . .'

'But?'

Crumble was looking at Fiddlesticks. She had climbed in among the wreck of the *Severed Head*. And worse, she'd fallen asleep. As easy as that. 'Oh, no!' But sleep's a flippin' funny thing. As soon as I looked at her I was yawning my head off. Suddenly, I was so tired I couldn't have saved the Lynth from Skeel or Kacasath if my life depended on it. (And it probably did). Huh, but us falling asleep isn't an adventure! What you want to know is what happened next. Well, yonks later, I was startled awake, by a sort of wet, bubbly, crackly noise.

The gargoyles and the nightmare were huddled anxiously together, close by. I sat up, before they noticed me. I could see Crumble's puzzled face, and Ulcie eagerly rummaging through the stuff in Fiddlesticks' canvas bag. That's where the noise was coming from. The radio was trying to speak to us again.

'Bisshi, currr currr, zzzzz zzzzz furrr furrr.' Couldn't understand a word of it.

'Oh, Billy, you're awake,' Ulcie wooed excitedly, holding up the radio. 'I think it's Mary. I think it's your Mary!'

'What?' I woke up properly then. And dragged Fiddlesticks awake with me.

'Ow, that hurt, Billy! What time is it?'

'Never mind the ruddy time, it's Mary—'

'Eh?'

'*Mary*. Mary, that is you, isn't it?' There were

more bubbling squeaks, and whizzes, and fizzes, and tiny blue electric flashes.

'Billy?' Fiddlesticks was rubbing her eyes, desperately trying to catch up. 'You mean, she's alive. Not killed in the Battle of Escareth?'

'Mary?' I yelled at the radio, and gave it a kick. (That didn't help).

'Ma-ry!' shouted Fiddlesticks, putting on her silly radio voice. 'If you can he-ar us p-lease say some-thing. O-ver.'

There was a sudden, distant flash of blue, not from the radio, but way out in the dirty, sludgy, purply-black sky. A blue the exact colour of the great mountain of Escareth. A low, murmuring growl followed the flash, and rumbled the whole length of the world.

Grimmack and Crumble huddled close together, and Ulcie gave a soft, worried woo.

'I think that was an answer,' I said. 'That was Murdle Clay, or Idrik Sirk at least, helping Mary. I'm sure. That was a 'Binder's magic.'

'What does it mean though? Is Escareth free?' Fiddlesticks twiddled her hair.

As if in answer, thunder roared. I mean really roared, out loud this time. The whole sky

181

streaked blue, then red, then green, then orange, and the radio crackled and spat some more of its gibberish, and began to smell a horrible, singey, electric smell.

'By the sound of all that lot, it's not just Escareth that's got itself free of Kacasath,' I said, hopefully. 'It's half of ruddy Murn!'

It didn't stay like that, though. It all went quiet, dark and smudgy again. But it had been a start. It was a sign to everyone: *things were happening*. Murn really was fighting back.

'Couldn't we just get our magic to take us to Escareth now, Billy? Y'know, to be with your Mary,' Fiddlesticks said. 'Murdle Clay could prob'ly put the Mam-thing right. 'Spect we could even be in the battles, if you want.'

'No, we couldn't,' I snapped, but I wasn't really angry. My heart was pounding in my head (it can, you know). 'We've got a hunt to finish. Our job's to stop Skeel and Kacasath. And at least while we're chasing that ruddy seaworm, we know she isn't leading armies against our Mary. That's got to be worth something.'

FOURTEEN

The Wild-goose Chase

Now it was a straight race. Us against them. Except of course, we didn't know where we were racing to!

'They'll have themselves a fair lead on us, blessem,' said Crumble. 'Cracked a pace, did Skeel. Seems his Mistress is gettin' the jitters, gettin' her coils in a twist.'

'Aye,' Grimmack said. 'Went so fast they did, nobody done noticed a pair o' broken old gargoyles hidin' themselves away.'

'Huh. I don't suppose they've stopped to fall asleep either!' I said.

We climbed slowly out of the valley, over the small hill, and down on to a flat, endless wilderness Ogrin had called the fourth mountain. (Didn't make any sense to me. Not yet anyway). More than once already we had glimpsed a distant group of figures – a short line of them, hardly six or seven strong – snaking their way slowly forwards. They were a long way ahead of us, a very long way ahead of us. But the dark stain, the sickly, gooey trail Kacasath left behind her was a cinch to follow.

'I'm thirsty, Billy,' Fiddlesticks said, sulkily. We had long since thrown away the last of the soggy sandwiches and drunk the pop (which had been all mixed up with sea water anyway). 'And I've got another rotten stitch, and a great big blister on my foot that's bound to go horribly septic.'

Fiddlesticks wasn't the only one with sore feet. Sharp stabs of pain jabbed me every time I took a step. I didn't tell her that, though. You see, in a funny kind of way, the pain helped me to keep going. Like I knew that if I stopped to rest, even for half a second, the pain would get a billion times worse, and I would never, ever, get started again.

'We *must* keep going,' I said.

'Well, I just *can't*. I can feel my heart pounding. I think it's going to explode!' She started to limp and clutched at her side. Doing her rotten amateur-dramatics bit. 'And we're never going to catch them up at this rate. Not ever.'

184

I felt like saying I'd leave her behind, but somehow it came out as, 'Please, Fiddlesticks, try. Please.' I took hold of her hand, lengthened my stride and dragged her with me.

'I'm going to die,' she whined. 'I am. Too much exercise isn't good for you. It's a well-known fact.'

'A boot up the backside isn't good for you either!' I said. Well, I'd had enough of her.

A lot, lot later . . . another glimpse of movement ahead. And later still, another. They were as far away from us as ever.

'And what happens if we find the Lynth first?' Fiddlesticks was *still* whingeing.

'First?'

'Before Skeel and Kacasath.'

'Huh, that's not very likely, is it?'

'We might. Nobody but Skeel has ever seen it. Anyone could easily run right past the Lynth and never even know.'

'You'd know,' Ulcie wooed, in a strange tone of voice I didn't really like. That's when all the moaning stopped. After that, we concentrated on following the nasty gooey stains, the withered, blackened trail Kacasath was leaving behind her. Plodded on through the wilderness in silence.

Except, it wasn't a wilderness at all. It really was another mountain. A huge mountain, almost as big as Escareth. Sounds daft, doesn't it? Well, it had taken me ages, but I'd finally worked it out. The wilderness *was* the fourth mountain of Aul'Jewen. But you see, a mountain that had toppled over, a mountain that was lying down flat, on its side. Sort of sad-looking, somehow.

At first, the ground we moved across was nothing but slabs of rock, as smooth and hard and unforgiving as the tarmac of a schoolyard. Loose pebbly stones followed the rock. Then patches of soggy clarts, covered with a yukky, mossy stuff that stuck to your feet, and stank like boys toilets. And then came the stands of tall, prickly, sticky plants, so thick with undergrowth we couldn't have explored them, even if we'd wanted to. 'Mizzle,' Ulcie wooed nervously when she saw them, and pushed us all quickly past, without explaining. The strangest thing though, was the way the wind blew across the fallen mountain. It howled down odd, narrow little holes, that ran right through the ground, for ever. (I dropped a pebble into one, and it never hit the bottom). And as the wind blew the mountain played soft tunes to itself. Not happy tunes, that would have been too much to ask for. Slow, sad, miserable tunes.

Then, more slabs of rock, more pebbly stones, more clarts and mizzle . . . and always following Kacasath's poisoned trail. Every now and again the seaworm's dirty tracks would thicken for a few steps, become dirtier, stickier, more disgusting than ever. But on we went, and on, and on . . .

'That's strange,' I said almost to myself, as I caught my breath for a moment.

'What's not strange,' Fiddlesticks puffed, 'what's not strange in this place?'

'All right, not strange. But odd, then. Dead odd.'

'What's dead odd?'

'Well, I'm sure we've just past the same patch of clarty ground for the second time.'

'Eh?'

'The same ground! I mean, it's not quite in the same place, more over to the left, when it

187

was over to the right last time – but it's still got my footprint in it! And that clump of mizzle, I've seen that before, too. And there – that tune – the mountain's playing the same tune I heard ages ago.' I suddenly realised I was whispering. Something wasn't right. Something was very, *very* wrong.

Ulcie wooed, worriedly.

'But surely that would mean Skeel is runnin' them all around in circles,' Crumble whispered back. 'On a wild-goose chase, blessem!'

'Why would he do that'n?' Grimmack asked, scratching his head. 'He's tryin' to catch the Lynth, in't he?'

'Oh, it doesn't make any sense, Billy. And I can't see any footprints, just a splodgy mess,' Fiddlesticks said. 'It's prob'ly just your silly imagination. Anyway, if we were going in circles we'd be walking on top of Kacasath's old trail marks, wouldn't we?'

'Well, maybe it's not proper circles, maybe it's more zigzaggy or spirals or something.'

'Yes, but—'

'And we *are* walking on top of her old marks. Don't you see? She keeps crossing over her own tracks. That's why they keep getting thicker and then thinner again.'

'Yes, but why hasn't anybody else noticed, then, Billy?'

'I don't know, do I. Maybe they're just not looking. Or, or maybe the Lynth's moving in zigzaggy circles too, so that's the way they've got to follow.' Huh, I admit it, I was guessing again, and nobody was believing me. 'Right then! Right. I'll ruddy well prove it to you.'

'What are you going to do,' Fiddlesticks said, 'stay here, until the hunt comes around again? Billy? *Billy?*'

Ulcie wooed, worriedly again, and Grimmack scratched his head with his foot. But I didn't answer. I just stood there, open-mouthed, my head pounding with excitement.

'Billy, what's wrong with you, what's the matter?' (I don't think I actually heard Fiddlesticks' words, just saw her mouth going.) You see . . . you see, she'd just told me how we could win the race, how we could beat Kacasath and Skeel, how we could reach the Lynth first. And it was a cinch! Fiddlesticks had tripped right over the answer head-first, and hadn't even noticed.

At last I got my voice back. 'Flippin' ruddy Norah! Don't you see? That's exactly what I'm going to do! I'm going to stay right here, and you're all staying with me! Let Skeel go chasing around in circles, dragging the seaworm with him! We'll be hiding here, waiting for the Lynth to come to us!'

We quickly hid ourselves. It was a good spot to hide. There were tall tats of scraggy weed that bowed and waved with the wind. And big lumps of rock, standing out on their own, like giant versions of the burnt stuff you find stuck to the insides of frying pans. And there were boggy clarts, and clumps of mizzle.

'Right. Nobody's to say another word,' I hissed. 'Not unless they see something, or hear something. I want complete silence!'

'Billy?'

'Oh, what is it, Fiddlesticks?'

'I was just thinking. What happens if the hunt's *not* travelling in circles, or spirals?'

'Eh?'

'I mean, what happens if you're wrong?'

I didn't have an answer to that one. I shushed her, and tried to ignore the feeling that was growing inside of me, the feeling that was like a lump of stodgy bread and butter pudding, weighing me down.

I just had to be right. I just had to be.

FIFTEEN

The Seaworm Gives a Lecture

Waiting, just waiting and nothing else, must be the hardest thing to do in the whole world. And we waited for ever! Yonks! There were no signs, though. No Lynth. No hunters. And what if I *was* wrong about the going-round-in-circles stuff? The longer we hid, the further away they all got.

'Maybe we've missed them, and we'll catch the Lynth the next time round,' Ulcie wooed hopefully, under her breath.

'No, I'm sure,' I said. 'I'm sure we haven't missed them.'

'Then where's the Lynth?' Fiddlesticks said, accusingly. 'We'll have to go after them. We'll have to try and catch them up.'

'No, it's too late for that. The hunt hasn't been round once yet. It hasn't. Not yet.'

'Well, p'haps that Skeel's already done caught y'un Lynth,' Crumble said. 'And they're never gettin' here, blessem.' As that awful thought struck home the bread and butter pudding in my stomach turned to solid cement.

And then, at last, I saw something. Just the tall grass buckling with movement, and a bit off to our left, instead of straight ahead. But real enough. '*There!* Did you see that?'

'Where, Billy? Where?' Fiddlesticks whispered through her teeth.

'Shush now, keep y'un eyes open, and listen up, blessem,' Crumble hissed.

We listened.

There was the sound of a voice, getting closer. It was a bit muffled and gurgling angrily, but I knew who *that* was. Kacasath, Kacasath the seaworm. And so close now I was sure she was on the other side of the rocks we were hiding behind. Huh, no Lynth. But we'd suddenly caught up with the hunters, and without even trying.

'What treachery is this? Am I the old woman's blind donkey to be lead by the nose? Eeeee Aaaaaw! Does the very ground not wither beneath my belly? Do not all but the foolhardy avoid my glance and call me Mistress? What simpleton would lead me across my own trail? You will pay for this outrage, treacherous friend. You will pay dearly. I will turn your blood sour in your veins, I will make your eyes boil inside your head. I will—'

That wasn't the end of it. No. She ranted and raved like that for ages and ages. But well, enough's enough. And anyway, I wanted a better look at what was going on.

Cautiously, I squirmed my way around the side of the rock, and poked my nose out through the weeds. I saw the seaworm at once. Kacasath's ancient withered body was coiled up tight. Her slimy, crooked tail whipped and lashed about angrily, oozing a sickening, pusy gunge everywhere, and her head was raised as if she was about to strike out. A few steps away, shuffling uneasily together, in a tight group, were the last five crew members of the *Severed Head*. (Two fat, ugly-looking goblins, one of the small nameless flitty things, an old hag and a very sad-looking rock troll). Standing close to the crew, but sort of deliberately on his own, was the snitch – Skeel.

Kacasath was yelling at them. *At them*.

'I don't understand. What's happening,

Billy?' Fiddlesticks had crept up beside me. I shook my head at her, did a quick mime of zipping her mouth shut.

Kacasath hadn't finished, but she had stopped ranting. Instead, she had uncoiled herself and was wriggling angrily, backwards and forwards. As she turned towards us I could see the beginnings of something like a smile breaking out across her face. That smile was worse than her curses. That smile could have cracked a hard-boiled egg a hundred thousand miles away.

'Would anyone care to own up? Care to explain? Offer themselves up to my *endless* mercy?' She was playing horrible games. Now she was trying to be nice, and that was almost as bad as her smiling. Her words were soft and coaxing, more poisonous than a snakebite.

Nobody shuffled now. Nobody dared.

'No? Hmmm, I thought not. Well, perhaps I can explain for you.' She stopped wriggling backwards and forwards and began to slither around them, carefully counting out loud, with each twist of her coils. 'One, two, three, four . . .'

'What's she up to?' Fiddlesticks whispered. (I used my hand on her mouth this time).

'Fifteen, sixteen, seventeen . . . oh look,' Kasacath suddenly gasped in mock surprise. 'Look at all those strange markings in the ground. Don't they look just like mine! I wonder how they got there?'

Silence.

'All right then, if that question is too difficult for you,' she was smiling again, 'let me cheer you up with a little riddle instead. I like riddles. When is a line not a line?'

Silence.

'When . . . is a line . . . not a line? Do you give up? Hmmm?'

She gathered up her answer word by word, carefully piled each one up on her tongue until they were all there. Then, she spat them out in one huge poisonous lump. 'WHEN IT'S A CIRCLE!' she bellowed. Her head seemed to move in twenty different directions all at once. Her lipless mouth split open, baring her teeth. Her nostrils flared, her eye grew large and threatening. And then, she suddenly fell quiet again. Too quiet. And her voice was a kitten's mew. 'Well, my faithful follower, my dutiful guide. What say you? Aye, you, Master Skeel, what say you?'

Skeel's nose twitched, once.

More silence. The wrong kind of silence. A dangerous silence that left you wishing she would start huffing and puffing again. A silence that waited patiently, dared even, dared anyone to speak and break it, so that she could bite out their tongue, take the offending head with it.

Well, there was one good thing, at least Kacasath hadn't seen us. She didn't know we were there.

'Billy . . . Billy Tibbet, are you there? Are you receiving me? You've just got to hear this—' The radio inside Fiddlesticks' bag was suddenly blaring at us, full blast. And clear as day!

'Oh, flamin' ruddy heck! Not now, Mary,' I yelled. 'Not now!'

SIXTEEN

The Dark Silent Pool

Kacasath roared her fury in words I didn't understand, and turned the air into a raging, swirling, sickly blue storm. Now that Mary's message had given us away, her argument with Skeel was instantly forgotten. The crew of the *Severed Head* scattered as Kacasath cursed again, jigged and ranted.

And then, she came wriggling towards us, squealing her contempt. The earth beneath her coils began to turn over: rocks, scrubby plants, everything. Boulders as big as buses were plucked right out, and thrown aside.

'Can't seem to keep my feet, blessem,' Crumble cried, as she and Grimmack collided, knocking great lumps off each other, sending each other crashing to the ground. The sea-worm gurgled with delight as we stumbled and fell about, as we tried desperately to stand up again.

'Fiddlesticks,' I bellowed. 'Fiddlesticks, we

must *do* something.' She was somewhere behind me, scrabbling about on all fours.

'Use your Firestones,' Ulcie cried out, as the squalling storm sucked her up into the air and spat her out again beyond our reach.

'Yes! Yes!' Fiddlesticks screamed, already reaching for hers. I tore my stone from the string around my neck, clenched it tight in my fist. 'Quick, Billy. Think! *Think!*'

Not quick enough! Kacasath was almost on top of us.

'Run for it, Fiddlesticks.'

'But, Billy—'

'Just run. Go on.' I tried to push her away, got ready to kick, to bite— And then, Skeel was there too. Skeel, standing in Kacasath's way, leaning over me, getting in first, pinning me to the ground. But what difference did it make? He could chop me up into tiny little bits just as easily as she could. I yelled out, screamed a name: his, I think, or maybe Fiddlesticks', I don't remember. Then . . . then . . .

I found myself staring into his eyes. His strangely blank, unseeing eyes, but, well . . . found myself looking far deeper than just my own reflection. It was as if I'd been plunged into a deep, dark, silent pool. And if I say Fiddlesticks was already in that pool, and so was our Mary, and my mam and dad, and the gargoyles, and oh, everybody else you can possibly think of – including Murdle Clay, Idrik Sirk and Kacasath, (yes, even the awful seaworm) . . . well then, you're just going to have to believe me. Even if it is impossible. Suddenly, I was certain I knew who Skeel was.

'Then, you're . . . *you're* the Lynth? You're the flippin' Lynth?'

I'm almost sure he spoke out loud, then. 'No, child. No, not I. Look deeper. Search those places where no eyes are needed to see, no ears to hear. Search there and understand.'

'But—'

'Myths and tales. Legends and imaginings. In those places you will find your Lynth – safe and sound, for none can hunt him there. Not man, not beast, or worm.'

'But, but—' But with that, the dark pool was gone.

Skeel had turned his back on me, was facing a very real-looking seaworm. And at last I did understand. I worked it all out, in that one split second. What better way was there of keeping Kacasath from conquering Murn than to have her running round in circles, chasing thin air, on a sort of never-ending dead-end hunt?

'Finished playing merry games then, Master Skeel?' Kacasath roared. She curled her lipless mouth into a smile that was worse than any threat.

Skeel's nose twitched, as if it sensed her awful smile, but he held his ground.

'Surely you are not such a fool?' For a moment Kacasath hesitated, as if she saw something in front of her that nobody else could see. 'Why bother yourself with these ridiculous children,' she said. Well, she didn't actually say it. She just looked with her one, hideous eye. But that's what she would have said, and I wasn't going to let her get away with it.

Fiddlesticks was busy crawling up my legs, trying to steady herself against me. 'Right,' I said. 'Are you ready with that stone?'

'Yes.'

No time to think this time, just—

201

Bzzzz-ZZzzooonnNKK!

The spell didn't work, not properly. What's new, eh? You see, at the exact moment we did our spell Kacasath did a spell of her own. But you know, if our attempt at magic didn't go right, then neither did hers. In fact, I think our spells must have got muddled up or something, got mixed in together somewhere in the middle, because they suddenly went off together with one enormous BANG!

I went sliding one way (backwards), Fiddlesticks went sideways, and the ground between us began to buckle and bend, twisting like a whirlwind. It broke into a million tiny little bits and shot up into the sky. There were plenty of special effects that went with it too: thunderflashes, streams of lightning and stuff. Whole flippin' firework displays.

It was another one of those times when I can never be quite sure what happened. And if that sounds like a swiz, then that's tough. I can't help it, I can only tell you what I know. When I stopped spinning around like a top, stopped being bashed by lumps of loose stones and that, stopped being zipped and zapped by rotten little bits of spilt magic, I found myself alone. I was clinging desperately to a small piece of rock, and had my eyes deliberately half-closed, so that I didn't have to look around me. Didn't have to see the rotten mess I was in.

So much for magic. Magic wasn't ever going to be my thing. It never got me anywhere. In the end, it wasn't anything the least bit magical that sorted things out. No, in the end it was just Fiddlesticks. Well, Fiddlesticks, Ulcie, and the Mam-thing.

I found my hand resting against the Mam-thing's jam-jar. (How I'd managed to carry it all that way without breaking it, I don't know). Anyway, I poked my hand inside, to make sure she was safe and that.

There was no Mam-thing.

'Mam?' I yelled. What a time to pick to make an escape. 'Mam, where are you?'

'Is that you, Billy?' The voice that answered was anxious and full of tears, but it wasn't Mam's.

My eyes were still half-shut, but I had to open them properly then. There wasn't any fourth mountain of Aul'Jewen, there wasn't any

Aul'Jewen. In fact, there weren't any mountains at all. Just smashed-up lumps of rock floating about in a purply-grey nothingness. Like bits of litter on a hot summer's day, left to blow about an empty park when all the visitors have gone home.

'Billy?' the voice called to me again, and then its owner floated gently past.

'Fiddlesticks, is that you?' I said. Of course, it was, and Ulcie too, holding on to her, keeping her in the air. 'Have you seen my mam anywhere? I think she's gone and done a bunk!'

'No, no, she hasn't, blessem.' This time the anxious voice was Crumble's. She and Grimmack drifted slowly overhead, clinging to their own slither of rock. They were both pointing, desperately jabbing fingers at the air. 'Billy, she's over there. OVER THERE!'

'Oh yes, yes. I see her. Mam?' I yelled. 'MAM! COME BACK, WILL YOU!' Huh, I couldn't *really* see her though. Well, not at first, anyway. Just more and more pieces of floating rock, and bits of tatty nettles, mizzle and stuff, gently dipping and bobbing in the air in time to each other – as if something very small and light was eagerly scuttling across them. The Mam-thing never stopped once. She leapt like an expert, from one object to the next. 'MAM!' I screamed again, 'Oh, Mam – where are you going?'

Huh. Then I saw where she was going.

There was one floating rock that was bigger than all the rest, and it was moving slowly towards us, its edges dripping a smelly, purply-blue gunge. Upon its highest point an unmistakable, crooked figure was watching us. *Kacasath*. And worse – a Kacasath coiled up, ready to pounce.

Well, the Mam-thing pounced first – was climbing up her withered tail, was underneath the rag-baggedy leathery cloth of her disgusting clothes.

'EEEEE!' Kacasath cried out. 'What's that? OOOOO! OW! ABA, ABA, OOOOK! EEEEE!'

'She sounds just like a monkey.' Fiddlesticks laughed out loud, and I couldn't help laughing with her. The air around the seaworm was turning an even deeper, murkier blue, as she thrashed about. 'GET – OW! OW! – OUT OF THERE! *What ever you are!*' Uncontrollable streaks of magic flew wildly everywhere. 'Na-na-na-NOOOOO! Don't you dare. Don't you dare. Not down there. NOT THERE! I'LL – I'LL–'

'Now's our chance, Fiddlesticks,' I yelled. 'We can stop her for good.' I felt for the Firestone around my neck. It wasn't there. Wasn't in my hand either. 'Oh, heck . . .'

'Billy?'

'Just do something, will you!'

'Can, can I help?' Ulcie wooed hesitantly, floating half a step towards me, half a step towards Kacasath.

'Yes, yes, go on then. Go on, the pair of you.'

'But what can we do?' Fiddlesticks cried.

'Oh, I don't know. Think of something. Anything. *Anything!*'

Well, that's exactly what they did. Anything. Ulcie opened her mouth as wide as it would go, and screamed. 'WWWWWWWOOOOOOOOO-OOOOOOO!' And then she dived, swooped down on Kacasath, took Fiddlesticks with her. All I could do was stand and watch. Fiddlesticks was still holding her piece of the Firestone in her hand, and . . . she threw it. And that's all she did.

Fiddlesticks Milligan threw her Firestone at Kacasath.

'Nooo!'

Nothing even faintly magic happened. The stone flew through the air, just like ordinary stones do. Then it hit Kacasath, hit her smack in the eye. She only had the one. It was enough.

I heard the seaworm squeal, and it was such a horrible twisted-up squeal I can't think of any way of describing it. I saw her turn, wriggling first towards Ulcie and Fiddlesticks as they swished past her a second time, doing a recky, and then, wriggling blindly towards me.

I saw her slither.

I saw her slip, and stumble.

Did I blink and was she gone? Or did I see her fall? Did she drop, head-first into the nothingness? Must have done. She left a trail of oily black gunge streaked across the sky, marking her fall. Her trail glooped and slooped and began to spread, leaking slowly across the already darkened skies, until darkness was everything.

Then, I remembered. 'Mam? MAM?'

SEVENTEEN

Lost in Space

'Are we ever going to get down from here, Billy? It must be days now, and I'm starving to death. Do you think that ocean might come back for us?' Fiddlesticks picked up the jam-jar, and rubbed her fingers thoughtfully across the glass, making it squeak. It was Crumble who had found the Mam-thing after the fight with Kacasath, in among the bits of debris and stuff. She was sleeping peacefully, now.

'Shhhhh. You'll wake her up,' I said. Well, it was better than trying to answer awkward questions. 'Mam's been through enough, so just leave her be.'

'I'm not waiting here for ever – marooned,' Fiddlesticks huffed. 'All of us, marooned in the middle of nothingness. Stuck to the same rotten piece of floating rock.' She stopped rubbing the jam-jar and gently cradled it instead. 'And I wish we still had the Firestone.'

'Yes, well, y'un haven't,' Grimmack chuckled, trying to be helpful.

'Or the radio!' (Fiddlesticks wasn't going to give in).

'Haven't got that either!' I snapped.

'We'll just have to wait an' see how Ulcie gets on, blessem,' Crumble said. Ulcie had formed herself into a one-nightmare search party, and had gone off alone, looking for survivors. Well, I was already sure there weren't any survivors. None of the left-over crew from the *Severed Head*, no seaworm, no Skeel. And for a moment I even wondered about the giant, Ogrin Thug.

Huh. Just us left. Just us.

It was about then that Fiddlesticks got all serious on me. 'Will you explain something to me, Billy?'

'What about?'

'You know. About Skeel, and the Lynth.'

To be honest, I didn't really know how to explain Skeel. So, I didn't. I just said, 'Look, Fiddlesticks, the whole Lynth thing, it was . . . it was *pretend*. A trick. Skeel was just pretending to hunt the Lynth. Just pretending to be on Kacasath's side all along.'

Fiddlesticks screwed up the bottom of her dress, and nodded in an empty-headed sort of way, like she was still puzzling something out.

I didn't know whether to laugh or cry. 'Oh, it's a cinch! There wasn't a *real* Lynth hunt, because . . . there isn't a real Lynth, because . . . Lynths are just mythical. It's like Fellin Tappa told us, right back at the start. And Skeel really was leading Kacasath on a wild-goose chase. Keeping her away from the battlefield, giving Murn a chance to fight back. And I'll bet Skeel wasn't the only one in on it, either.' I stopped, looked deliberately at the gargoyles. But Grimmack and Crumble just squirmed, and turned guiltily away.

Fiddlesticks had stopped twiddling with her dress, and was looking at me purposefully. 'What I want to know, Billy, is where do we come into all this? I mean, if the Lynth is just pretend, then we were chasing after Kacasath for nothing! We could have been helping your Mary with her battles all along.'

Huh, I was back to filling in the gaps with guesses again. 'Well, I think we're here to . . . to make things look good. You know, if the seaworm got the idea somebody else was after the Lynth, too – somebody desperate enough to come right out of another world, specially – well, it would make the whole pretend look that much more real.'

'Hmmm,' Fiddlesticks said thoughtfully, waggling her feet over the edge of our rock. 'But, Billy, it hasn't really worked, has it?'

'Eh?'

Fiddlesticks was looking around us. There we were, sitting on our rock in the middle of a smudgy-black nothingness, with no sign of Murn anywhere.

Huh, she was right again.

EIGHTEEN

Mary's Last Message

I don't know who heard the noise first. I don't suppose it matters.

A crackle . . . a crackling, fizzing poppiness. 'Did you hear that, Fiddlesticks?'

'Yes. Yes, I did.'

The gargoyles suddenly stood up, and turned anxiously towards the noise. (As if that was going to help them hear it better!) 'Coming from down there, blessem,' said Crumble.

'No, no,' chuckled Grimmack. 'It's up a bit.'

'Shush, will you,' I said. 'Shush! And listen.'

'. . . Crackle . . . Spit, spat . . . Crackle . . .'

'Gettin' closer, blessem.'

'Louder.'

'Can't see anythin', though.'

'*Can*!' I snapped. 'Can see something!'

'Wooooooo hooooo!' wooed Ulcie bursting with excitement. 'Wooooooo hooooo.' She came whooshing towards us, carrying something in her hands. 'I've found it. I've found it.' She floated down on to our rock and plonked the radio in my lap. Or rather she plonked the few bits of tat, the plastic cover, and the crumpled electric-looking things that were all that were left of the radio, in my lap.

'Is it still working?' she wooed, anxiously. Well, by rights it shouldn't have been. But it was, in a way.

'Just snap, crackle an' pop,' Grimmack chuckled.

'All busted an' broken, blessem,' tut-tutted Crumble.

'That's never going to work again.'

'Fizz . . . crackle . . . Pip, pop—'

'Can you hear something, Billy?'

'Shhh,' I hissed.

'Snick . . . Snack . . . Spap, Spip—' Then, at last, I heard Mary's voice, fainter than a whisper. 'Hello . . . Hello . . .'

'Batteries runnin' down,' Grimmack chuckled (until I glared at him).

'Hello . . . Are you there? Anybody?'

'Yes!' I yelled.

'Snap . . . Snip . . . Snap . . .'

213

'Yes!' I yelled again, and this time, everyone yelled with me.

'Billy . . . Is that you? You're very faint. Can't you speak up a bit?'

'Yes!' we all yelled again, even louder. 'Flippin' well, yes!'

'Oh, Billy, Billy, you're safe. And Mam?'

'Yes, she's here.' Fiddlesticks held the Mam-thing's jam-jar up to the radio, as if to prove it.

'I was beginning to think . . . I thought, I . . .' Our Mary got all soppy and stuff then, so I won't bother with that, just skip to the good bit. 'Oh, but I've got some wonderful news.'

'Have you?' we yelled.

'Murdle Clay has won. Touch and go, until that awful Kacasath was properly out of the way, but she's done it, in the end! And Murn is free – *free*!'

'Is it?' we yelled, looking very doubtfully at the dark streak of nothingness all around us.

'Couldn't have done it without Idrik, of course.'

'Oh, of course.' Me and Fiddlesticks were pulling faces at each other, in disbelief.

'Oh, Billy. There were some really horrible

battles! But everyone helped – the flying pigs – and Brock and Fellin Tappa – and the rock trolls – and the snooks and the dragons – and oh, just everyone! . . . Fzzzz . . . Snit . . . Snat . . . Fzzzzzzz . . .' The radio was beginning to fade away, again. 'And now . . . the 'Binders are putting Murn back the way it should be. And oh, fo – fuur fuur fu fu . . . Better go, Billy. The spell's weakening. I'm sending an old friend to fetch you . . . Snip . . . Snap . . . Crack . . . Zzzeee zzuu zu zu . . .'

Silence.

'Mary?' we yelled. 'MARY!'

Well, that's just typical of our Mary. She gets all the good stuff, even in adventures. The proper battles, the flying pigs, the *real* Spellbinders and everything. And me? Fiddlesticks Milligan, Kacasath the seaworm, and a flippin' wild-goose chase.

Then, something else happened. The veil that had been cloaking the sky around us – Kacasath's poisonous trail – began to break up. First, a tiny yellow crack of light spilled through (the moon, I think). And then, like bedroom curtains drawn back on to a glorious summer's day, the whole thing fell away.

'Oh, Billy!' Fiddlesticks cried. 'What is it? What is it? It's so beautiful.'

'Murn,' I said. 'It's Murn. The real Murn.'

You're probably wondering what this Murn looked like. Well, it's stupid fairy-tale stuff, again. You know, the ninety-seven mountains all back in one piece and that. All shining silvery-gold, all bright reds, coppers, and greeny. And there, right in the middle, standing proudest of all, was the blue mountain of Escareth. Murdle Clay's mountain.

Some of the mountains looked just like, well, just like mountains. But lots more were like Gorgarol: huge mountain-castles or cities, with twisting towers instead of peaks. All windows and doors, terraces and orchard gardens. There was an ocean too, lapping gently at the feet of Escareth, sparkling like diamonds under the full moon. Here and there, the mountains had rivers running their full lengths, top to bottom. Off the bottom even! And the river water fizzed and splashed about, and made babbling noises that sounded just like gentle crying. But crying with laughter.

'Billy, can we go there, now?' Fiddlesticks said in a quiet voice, after we had sat and watched for ages.

'Dunno,' I said.

Fiddlesticks, Grimmack, Crumble, and Ulcie – they were all looking at me. 'Dunno,' I said again. 'I dunno.' Well, I didn't.

''Spect Murdle-what's-it will turn the Mam-thing back into your proper mam,' Fiddlesticks said, hopefully.

''Spect so.'

''Spect someone'll come and rescue us, too. Like Mary said.'

''Spect they will.'

Almost on cue, tiny wisps of smudgy, foggy mistiness began to lap around us, sliding in and out of our rocks. The tiny wisps began sticking together. Making themselves into one great big smudgy, foggy mistiness.

'Billy, what's happening?' Fiddlesticks squeaked. Ulcie wooed nervously and got herself ready to faint, just in case.

I stood up, stepped forward, almost to the edge of our rock, determined to get between it – whatever *it* was – and Fiddlesticks. Grimmack and Crumble stepped forward with me.

But it wasn't just a misty cloud. No. Something very real was beginning to take shape. A horse and a rider?

'Don't come any closer! You don't scare us with your rag-baggedy tricks. I'm warning you,' I yelled, making fists, stamping my feet.

The shape came no further. Stood half-lost in the mist. And then it spoke.

'Ka! What kind of welcome is this, boy? What kind of welcome for foot-weary travellers? Did this kelpie carry my burden all this way, just to be insulted?'

'Kelpie? But – Idrik? Idrik Sirk, is that you?' I still couldn't see them properly. 'Is that really you?'

'Urgh, Billy, I'm going to be sick. He really is a rotten skeleton,' Fiddlesticks squeaked, twisting up the bottom of her dress, almost losing her voice with the shock. 'A rotten, dead skeleton!'

'Oh, I am, am I, girl?' said Idrik Sirk, and his voice could have been a howling wind, blowing under old floorboards, in a dark empty house. 'Ka, well, maybes you're right! And maybes I'm such an awful apparition I should just go away again, without you?' He was suddenly laughing.

'No, please, please stay,' Ulcie wooed (making sure she was still well behind me). Well, Idrik Sirk didn't go away. He laughed again, and climbed down from the back of his mount. Then, he clack-clacked his bony way out of the mists, and across our rock.

'Ka! How goes it, old friend?' he said, with laughter ringing in his voice. Huh, he didn't mean me, though. Didn't bother with me, at all. And with that, Crumble threw her arms around him, and wouldn't let him go again. And then Grimmack joined in.

Well, I might have taken the huff, but you know, I didn't. You see, from the moment Idrik Sirk had said kelpie, my mind had been racing sixty to the dozen. I just left them to their hellos and stared into the wispy mists, trying to get a better look at whatever it was hiding there.

I wasn't imagining it, was I? I mean, Idrik Sirk was there, a real Spellbinder, even if he was dead. So . . . so why not?

The kelpie whinnied gently, and shook his great mane. Not just empty shapes in a windblown cloud. Not just a steamy, billowing, messiness of nothingness. *Our kelpie*. Tarn. Big, strong, powerful, and alive. Very much alive. He kicked out with his hooves, turned himself towards us, and into the moonlight. He wasn't just any old water kelpie, either. He was a sort of special, air-bound kelpie. A sort of cloud kelpie, that could fly and everything! Huh, when we'd done our sunny spell, maybe we'd actually done something right for once.

He took two, three great joyous leaps across the sky. Turned around and leapt back again, just for the fun of it.

'Is it really him, Billy?' Fiddlesticks asked.

Tarn answered for himself. 'No,' he said. 'No. It's somebody else.' Then he winked, and splashed us with moonlight.

Beside me, Fiddlesticks was crying. I didn't say anything. Didn't blame her. Not this time.

And now, we're nearly at the very end. Nearly.

'We'd best be setting off then, boy,' Idrik Sirk

said, his draughty voice serious again, now that all the hellos were done.

'Eh? But there's only one kelpie,' Fiddlesticks said. 'There's far too many of us for just him. And I'm not staying behind, not this time. Just don't bother to ask.'

Ulcie wooed anxiously, and Grimmack rubbed his broken arm.

'Ka!' cried Idrik Sirk. 'A dead 'Binder I might be, girl, but I still have my uses!' He might have twitched a bony finger, or it might have been a pure fluke. Anyway, there was suddenly a small flock of squawking, squeaking flying pigs, flapping their way eagerly towards us. Four, five, *six* pigs in all. And then, behind them, two more. There was Fellin Tappa upon a large grey . . . and, and there was . . . there was *our Mary*! Our Mary riding Brock, and all dressed up like a flippin' queen or something, laughing and joking and yelling at us to hurry on up!

There were no second thoughts. The first group of flying pigs were no sooner arriving than they were leaving again, with two chuckling gargoyles and the bony old Spellbinder on their backs. Our Mary didn't even wait for me!

Just set off again with Brock and Fellin Tappa, determined to lead the way like she was in charge.

'Ka! Jump on then, boy, jump on. Or are you staying up here for ever?' cried Idrik Sirk, as his flying pig began to wheel through the sky. Then he touched a finger to where his nose should have been, in a thoughtful, knowing way. ''Spect there's old friends to visit, and certain things still waiting to be put right.'

'Oh–' It was only then that I remembered about Mam. 'Oh, flippin' heck. Come on, Fiddlesticks, and bring that ruddy jam-jar with you.'

Huh, Fiddlesticks pushed the jam-jar at me, grabbed hold of Tarn's mane and pulled herself on to his back. Pulled me up behind her.

'Bye for now, blessem,' Crumble cried, waving from the back of her flying pig, as its wings began to beat. And Grimmack chuckled, and waved with her.

We waved back, yelled our goodbyes. And then, at last, Tarn began his dive . . .

'Weeeeeeeee!' Fiddlesticks screamed with delight.

I turned around, looked back over the kelpie's tail. Someone was stealing a ride, again. 'Don't you ever give up?' I said.

'You never know when you might need a rearguard,' Ulcie wooed. I just laughed. Laughed and hugged the Mam-thing's jam-jar, hugged it tight.

'Weeeeeeeee!' Fiddlesticks screamed again, between hicks of laughter. My insides turned slowly upside down and round the wrong way, as everything around us went whooshing past in one great big blurry slop. Behind me, Ulcie flapped along like a flag in the breeze.

And did we ever get to visit Murdle Clay? Did we get the Mam-thing turned back into our proper mam? And did we all get safely home again? Well, yes, of course we did. Of course we did, stupid.

But you know, when I think about it properly, that ride down through the skies of Murn, with the moonlight dancing across the kelpie's back, and the bright blue mountain of Escareth beckoning us on far below, that was where *my* adventure really ended . . . the second time.